DUNCAN JEFFERSON

THE BUTCHER'S BOY

I0592848

The Renaissance Brothers
✦ BOOK 1 ✦

Printed in the United States of America
First Printing, 2017

Printed in the USA

Cover by Jenn Reece at
WWW.TIGERBRIGHTSTUDIOS.COM
Interior design and typesetting by Write Dream Repeat Book Design
WWW.WDRBOOKDESIGN.COM

9 8 7 6 5 4 3 2 1

Paperback ISBN: 978-0-6480694-2-3

1

THE BUTCHER'S BOY

IT WAS ONLY a small twig, but when it snapped in the silence of the morning, it made a big noise. The sun had just begun to lighten the eastern sky, driving out the blues from the shadow of the hills, crowning them with the golden glow of day. The boy and his father had been watching a rabbit that hearing the sound, froze in place, listening. Nervous, it lifted its head while twitching its nose, as if testing the breeze for some hidden danger.

The rabbit heard the tiny twig snap when the careful boy shifted his weight. Fear sparked in its eyes, followed by the same look of fear in the boy's eyes. In a blink, the rabbit was secure in the recesses of its warren, but the boy's reflexes were too slow to avoid his father's hand. It crashed down on the side of his head, knocking him to the ground.

"You little fool!" the wild man seethed.

Raising his fist again, he managed to control his temper and yell.

"Get out of here! Go on, snivel off home to your mother and see what she has in store for you. And don't forget to tell her why you've been sent back empty-handed, you good-for- nothing wretch!"

As the boy scrambled to his feet, his father's parting kick sent him tumbling down the slope and into the bramble bushes below.

The man called his dogs to heel, and kneeling down to give them a gentle rub around the neck, he pointed them in a new direction. Meanwhile, the boy disentangled himself from the briars, climbed to his feet, and turned back toward the small village where he lived. He wasn't visibly upset by the event, because the same sort of thing happened to him almost every day. His parents treated him like a slave, and he knew that, while the boot in the backside hurt a little, his mother's punishment might be worse.

Rosso was the second son of six children. The firstborn son, Bastiano, was a true chip off the father's bitter, gran-ite-hearted block. A mini tyrant whose main vocation in life was to make his red-headed brother's life as miserable as possible, he was short and stocky, with jet-black hair and brown eyes—typical of the Venetians who lived in the area.

A plume of red hair heralded Rosso's birth, followed by the pale white skin of his little body. His father disliked him at first sight and made him the scapegoat of the family from that moment on. After Rosso, four girls were born in quick succession—all with their parents' black hair and dark, flashing eyes.

Although the girls began their lives with plump limbs and full voices, the first three must have decided that life in that family was not for them. When diphtheria arrived in the village, their spirits returned to their heavenly maker, leaving only the boys and the baby of the family to struggle on. Perhaps it was the baby Anna's stubbornness to live that triggered the red-headed Rosso's deep attachment to her. His parents often left him to hold her and nurse her through the illness.

"Because that way, ye're far more likely to catch it yerself and die," his big brother leered.

Rosso adored Anna, and when she was able to walk, she seemed to delight in him, following him everywhere. She was the only comfort he had in his early years—enough to keep his heart happy and his mind hopeful.

The children were an odd sight in and around the village: the taller, skinnier red-haired boy and the fine-boned, black-haired beauty, who followed him. Secretly, the locals believed that perhaps one day they'd wake up and everything would be fine. They knew the children's father well. If the children were in his way, then heaven help them!

"Butcher by name, bully by nature," neighbors whispered behind his back. Many had seen little Rosso limping along, carrying telltale bruises or showing other signs of the beatings he suffered at his father's hands. Yet the villagers did nothing. Perhaps it was because they lived in fear of the father, or it was because they needed the meat he sold them when food was scarce throughout the Republic. Because they did nothing, the sight of Rosso and his little sister was a source of great discomfort, paining their consciences.

So Rosso began his life believing that oppression was the natural state. Survival meant being inconspicuous and taking beatings in silence. Attempts at retaliation made things much worse.

As Rosso walked home, he thought of ways to escape the certain beating that his mother would dispense when he told her why he'd been sent home early. He considered lying to her. However, past experience taught him that being deceitful would only delay the inevitable. When the lie was found out, the beating would be even worse.

As Rosso approached the outskirts of the huddle of hovels that made up the small village, he passed a cart, carrying a coffin, headed toward the small cemetery at the edge of the community. He blessed himself with the sign of the cross. From early age, it was a frequent ritual he practiced.

Fever and disease were the constant companions of those who lived in and around the lagoons. Malaria seemed to come and go with the swarms of flies and mosquitoes that thrived in the area. It seemed as if plague, smallpox and the sweating sickness accompanied the people who passed through the busy seaport of the Venetian Republic.

✤ ✤ ✤

Rosso arrived at home, which was a small cottage with small mean windows that looked like half-shut eyes, with their overhanging shutters. A rotting cart, wreathed in weeds, stood where the garden should have been. A gap in the front fence indicated where the discarded gate had once, but no one ever entered the house by that door. A broad track swept around the side of the cottage, where low-roofed barns frowned in the distance, filling the air with a foul smell.

On that side of the cottage, an open half-door to the kitchen glared across the yard at the barns. Taking a deep breath, Rosso entered and found his mother seated in her favorite chair in the kitchen. She looked thin and pinched, with a deep color in her cheeks. Despite her weakened state, her eyes bored through him.

"What're you doing home so early?" she demanded, venom in her voice.

Looking down at his bare feet, Rosso told her how the rabbit had run away and how his father had blamed him. He looked up, expecting to see his mother fly into a rage. In fact, she reached for a cane and attempted to rise to make a dash at him. Exhausted however, she slumped in the chair.

"Just wait until your father gets home. He'll give you the beating of your life!"

As her head fell forward, she closed her eyes, gasping for breath and breaking out in a sweat.

"Are you all right?" Rosso asked. "Can I get you any-thing, Mama?"

"You can get out of my sight!" she snarled at him. "It's *your* fault that I got this fever! You'll be the death of me yet."

Rosso lifted the latch, careful to remain quiet, and went outside.

"Mamma's not well, is she?" a little voice asked from behind him.

He smiled when he turned, knowing it was Anna.

"No, she's not," he answered, lifting her into his arms. "What do you think we should do about it?" he asked, amused that he, her big brother, should be asking this wise young child what he should do.

"Do you think she's going to *die*?" she asked with a seri-ousness that shook him.

Although death was commonplace for every family in the area, it never occurred to him that his father or mother might die before him. Anna sought reassurance in his eyes.

"Perhaps I'd better get a priest," he said.

Putting her down, they marched off, hand-in-hand, to the monastery.

In rural areas, the rhythm of life followed the seasons, and the seasons were in the hands of God. It was what the Church taught, so the people believed it. Everyone was happy to live by God's law, and the keepers of his law, the followers of that poor, wise Saint Francis of Assisi, lived at the local monastery. Each day, the community of monks said their prayers, worked and helped the poor and vul-nerable. Not a minute of their time was wasted—from the time Brother Sun came up until Sister Moon sent him him to rest!

By most monastic standards, it was a modest building, next to a small chapel with a loud, clear bell. It was there that the three brothers lived out their vows, working and praying together, baptizing babies, marrying lovers and burying the dead. They had a small patch of land behind the house where they managed to grow seasonal vegetables, harvested olives from old gnarled trees and cared for old or feeble sheep that others had abandoned.

Brother Damien answered Rosso's knock and invited the children into the cool interior of the house. The building had four small rooms, or cells, for the brothers. The children stood in a the reception room next to a communal kitchen. It was a spare, bare room, with the sole decoration being a carved depiction of the Christ in his final agony.

Damien had a kind face, with mild eyes. His chin was small, as if it had been left behind in his rush to be born, giving him a somewhat simple appearance.

"It's a bit unusual for young folk to be about so early," he said in a high, lilting voice. "How can I help you children?"

Fearful, Rosso found himself choking back tears.

"It's our Mum. I think she's really sick with the sweating sickness, and we're not sure what to do. Dad's out hunting, and we can't disturb him while he's doing that, otherwise..."

His voice trailed off as he looked sidelong at his young sister, who reached up to hold his hand. Damien was new to the area, but even he had heard the village gossip, gleaning details about what went on in the butcher's household from the confessions of others in his small flock. *And so*, he thought, *now these two lost and confused children are right here.*

"So would you like me to come and see what I can do?" he asked in a compassionate tone.

"Yes please," they answered in unison.

The simple bond between them filled the monk with emotion.

"We don't want her to die!" Anna pleaded.

"I'll do all that is humanly possible to help her," he answered. "And then we'll leave the rest up to God."

Brother Damien took Anna by the hand, and the three left the monastery.

Striding up to the seldom-used front door, they entered and went straight to the kitchen, where the children left their mother. The chair was overturned, but there was no trace of her.

"You children wait in here. I'll call you in a minute."

The monk went to the door, his eyes searching the yard.

"What's wrong?" Rosso asked as he put a protective arm around Anna.

"Just wait in here until I call for you," the monk scolded as he closed the door.

He turned back to where the woman lay on the ground, a small pool of bloodied vomit smearing her face and fouling the dusty earth around her head. Her breathing was slow and came in great gulping gasps, leaving her body limp and flaccid. With each isolated breath, the air that left her lungs evaporated into eternity, an eternity into which her soul would soon follow.

The monk knelt at her side, smoothing the hair back from her face, and taking a cloth from his pocket, he wiped the vomit away from her blue-tinged lips. She heaved to breathe from leaden lungs as he whispered words of absolution into her ears and prayed that her final suffering would be short and swift.

His faith was strong. He'd been a companion of death for all his religious life, so he knew the woman was nearing the end of her earthly life. In the more grounded recesses of his mind, a small voice whispered, *she's going to have a lot of explaining to do when she meets her maker.* He spoke the final blessing out loud, "Ut custodiant te et ducet ad vitam Iesu Christi" words that roused Rosso to open the door to see what was happening. He knew his mother was dead as soon as he saw her, and he was surprised at how little emotion he felt.

Anna's reaction, however, was different. She approached her mother's motionless body, knelt at her side and caressed her face. Silent tears streamed from the girl's eyes, mixing with the dust on her face.

"I'm so sorry, Mummy," was all she said, and then she laid her head on her dead mother's chest.

The monk rose to his feet, watching the scene. Rosso stood over his little sister, like a silent sentinel. He prayed for tears of regret, as all sons should experience at a mother's death, but Heaven was silent, leaving his heart cold and empty.

After a moment, the monk knelt, lifted Anna to her feet, and led the children back into the house, giving instructions for Rosso to get a blanket.

"And I need you to go tell the neighboring women. They will come and attend to your mother's body to prepare it for her final service here on Earth."

The monk stayed in the kitchen, comforting Anna, who was wiping the tears from her face with a shirt sleeve.

Looking up at the monk with wise eyes, she asked, "Why did God make Mummy die? I know she wasn't a very good Mummy, and poor Rosso suffered so often at her hands and from the cruel things she used to say about him. But she was still our Mummy, wasn't she? I just don't understand?"

"I can't give you an answer to that question," he answered. Pausing to reflect, he continued. "It's a bit like being in a very dark cave—it's really scary, and you can feel all alone, but you must realize that just outside the cave, the sun is shining or the wind is blowing, though you can't see or feel that."

He wiped a tear from her face.

"One day, you'll understand. One day, you'll realize that you have to seek the sunlight and find where the wind is blowing. Now, it's all right to cry for your Mummy, because you'll miss her, but one day, you'll be able to love her in a way that perhaps you never could when she was alive."

As he looked at her, he saw the light of understanding in her face, filling his heart with wonder.

The sound of voices in the yard returned their thoughts to the present. Then an older woman ushered Rosso into the house under her sheltering arm.

"That's not a proper place for a lad to be, Brother," she said with an admonishing gaze.

Turning her back with a righteous readjustment of her shawl, she exited the kitchen, leaving the monk, Rosso and Anna standing there, wondering what to do next.

"Let's go out the front and wait for your father to return," the monk suggested. "And I'll wait with you until then, just to be sure."

There was a sort of dance involved when looking after the newly dead, a practice that involved the coming and going of several older women, the carrying back and forth of several jugs of water and the appearance of food and drink for the kitchen.

"Death is hard work," one of the women explained. "Especially for those left behind."

The words were uttered whilst she entered the kitchen door backward, holding a jumble of assorted plates and jugs. Soon, more neighbors appeared, accompanied by some of the menfolk of the community, but there was still no sign of Lundardo, the dead woman's husband.

By the time Rosso and Anna's father arrived home in the late afternoon, carrying several dead animals over his shoulder, he was well aware of the sound of raised voices coming from his kitchen. The dogs followed, and Bastiano brought up the rear carrying the knives, nooses and traps that were so necessary to killers of beast and man.

As Lundardo entered the yard, he ignored everyone and veered off toward the butchering room where he stored his carcasses. Brushing past the crowd, he scanned the scene through narrow feral eyes. When he arrived at the shed, he dropped the carcasses and cleaned his bloodied blade on his coat sleeve before ordering the young tyrant to hang all the dead animals and drain their blood into jars. Then he turned to go back to the house.

✠ ✠ ✠

Brother Damien had been observing him and met him halfway across the yard.

"I'm afraid I have some bad news for you," he said.

The man glowered at him.

"I knew that kid would come to no good. Serves him damned well right! What's he done this time?"

As the monk reached out to touch the butcher's arm, the butcher pulled away, taking defensive step backward.

"*Not* the little un?" he asked, attempting to interpret the holy man's facial expression.

For the first time, the butcher's face showed anxiety and concern.

"No," the monk replied. "It's your wife. I'm afraid she's dead. There was nothing any of us could do to save her. She didn't suffer," he added in a soft voice.

In most evil men, there is often one redeeming feature. In the butcher's distorted view of life, he had truly loved his wife. The misfortune was that he could only express such love was through violence. His formative experience of family love had come from his father, who beat his wife—and his son too. It had never crossed his mind for a moment that there might be other, less destructive ways to express love. Now his love was dead, and the hard shell that surrounded his heart cracked for a moment, exposing the grief that overwhelmed him at the shock of her death.

"She wasn't that sick when I left this morning," he moaned like a deranged beast, standing there with wide, open eyes, appearing confused and lost.

However, that tiny crack snapped shut, and his eyes narrowed once again.

"Why didn't anyone *tell* me? Where's that useless idiot of a son? Why didn't he come to me when he knew she was so sick? Just wait till I get my hands on him!"

He was searching for the hilt of his knife when the monk stepped in front of him, like David had stood before Goliath. Brother Damien struck him between the eyes with the power of unexpected words.

"The boy could do nothing! She was dead before he got here," he hissed through his teeth, right into the face of the butcher, who was staggered by the unlikely adversary. The small man with the small chin had a huge heart, and he was armed with an irresistible might. Taking a step toward his bewildered foe, he continued.

"That child is a better man now than you have ever been, or will ever be, so leave him alone!"

The impassioned monk's words crushed the butcher, who was already dazed by the unexpected death of his wife. Listening from behind the door of the storage room, Bastiano overheard the conversation, and the words he heard only made him despise Rosso even more.

"That devious brat," he muttered to himself. "It's all his fault," he said as he punched a dead rabbit in the face. From that moment on, he began to think of ways to make his brother's life even more miserable.

2

THE BEGINNING OF THE END OF THE BEGINNING

THE VILLAGERS held her burial in the Christian tradition. The sight of two young children holding each other's hands was moving to many present. Others were aggrieved at the sight of the son who stood by his broken father. The community gathered around the mother's grave, listening as the stoney clay rattled the wooden lid of the coffin, whilst the priest said the final blessings and goodbyes. With the rites concluded, the villagers returned to their homes, and by the next day, they were immersed in the daily rounds of work and family life. The butcher and his family were alone.

As the months passed, the butcher took to wine and got drunk every day. His effete state did not make Rosso's life any easier, because his brother took on the mantle of chief tormentor. At the age of fourteen, he was a stocky, powerful teenager who saw himself as the man of the house, his faded father having handed over more and more of the business. His father's capitulation also left him free to torment and boss around his weaker brother from morning to night.

One night during that bitter time, Rosso closed the door of the foul outhouse where the rotting bones were stored. He walked a few paces and slumped to the ground in the darkness, lying on his back to look at the stars. The bruised meadow grass beneath his body released eddies of scents into the air around him. It was cool and fresh outside, and he thought he wouldn't be missed, because his brother decreed that he should eat his meals outside, "with the other dogs."

Anna never forgot her red-headed brother, and Rosso felt her presence before he saw her. Without saying a word, she lay down with her head next to his. They stared into the heavens for a moment before she spoke.

"Did *God* put all those stars up there, Rosso?"

"That's what they say," he answered, not wanting to dampen her innocent faith.

"And is it true that he puts a new one up there every time someone dies?" she asked in a little voice.

"That's what they say," he answered again.

"Does that mean that there's one up there for Mummy too?"

Rosso couldn't answer straight away. He couldn't speak because of the large lump in his throat and the tears forming in his eyes. But that moment of silence was beautiful between them, and no words were needed.

"Do you think God will put a star up there when I die?" she asked.

Rosso turned his head to find her wise eyes and whispered into her ear.

"It'll be the most beautiful star the world has ever seen!"

He reached over, squeezing her hand. She continued, after a pause.

"Do you ever think of running away from home, Rosso?"

"Don't you ever stop asking questions?" he replied, as they giggled under the benevolent canopy of the night sky.

"It's time for your bed," he said to her offering her his hand and pulling her to her feet. He gave her a kiss and a hug.

"God bless you, little sister, and may he keep you safe. If you weren't here…"

He left the rest of the sentence suspended in that starlit moment.

Winter came early that year, and with it a new form of the sweating fever. It swept through the little community, claiming loved ones in many homes. The chinless priest was busy nearly every day with burials or blessings, but he never complained, and he would not refuse to attend a home, whether day or night, in snow or rain. *How he survived the onslaught caused by that silent killer only his Maker would ever know!*

Rosso was the first in his family to get sick. His brother had locked him in the storehouse, full of rotting bones and foul flesh. He began to cough on the very next day.

"He's putting it on," Bastiano told their father who was slumped over the kitchen table, an empty carafe rolling noisily by his elbow.

"But it ain't no point asking *you* what to do. You ain't in no bleeding shape to do anything anyway," he said, mocking the hollow husk who once had been his father.

His father tried to rear up with a semblance of paternal authority, but he merely succeeded in losing his balance before falling to the floor, where he lay moaning before passing into a drunken sleep.

"Now look what you've done," the tyrant said, leering at his little brother, advancing.

Rosso could hardly focus on his menacing sibling, as with each coughing fit, his head threatened to explode. Sweat coursed down the lower parts of his back and between his buttocks. He couldn't ever remember feeling so sick. The last thing he remembered was Anna arriving and standing between the two of them, like a white light between two poles of darkness. Then he stopped knowing anything.

He woke up in a small room with whitewashed walls. There was a small, high window through which he could make out that it was daylight, although the tiny patch of sky he saw seemed grey. He raised himself on one elbow, looking around. There was a rush mat on the floor and a small crucifix mounted above the bed.

He felt dizzy, and lying back, he fell asleep. He dreamed he was a white monk on a big black horse. In his dream, he was holding a huge sword and screaming at the top of his lungs, whilst galloping full tilt at a young man with a smiling face. There was a woman behind him on the horse, and she was shaking him by the shoulder, pointing towards a huge eagle circling overhead. He turned to tell her to stop shaking him so hard, worried that they'd both fall off.

Then he became aware that he was being roused from his dream by someone pressing him on the shoulder.

"Rosso, Rosso, are you awake yet... Rosso?" the voice repeated.

Opening his eyes, he saw the chinless monk and smiled.

"That's good," said the saintly man, although his sad expression seemed to be weighed down with a heavy burden. "Sit up, young man. I've got some broth for you. It'll help you get your strength back."

Putting a strong arm behind young Rosso's back, he lifted him forward and gave him a bowl of thin soup. The boy needed no second asking and soon drained the bowl until they could both see the grain of the wood at the bottom. Seeing the look of satisfaction on the monk's face, he turned his pinched features towards him.

"Do you know, father?—that's the best bowl of soup I've had in my whole life!"

The monk seemed shaken and aggrieved by his words.

"Tomorrow, I think you'll be well enough to get up, and then we'll have a chat together, just you and I."

He smiled and gave the boy his benediction before leaving.

Rosso called out just as the door was closing.

"How's the rest of my family? I hope they didn't catch what I've just had."

The only reply he received was the metallic click of the latch as it closed.

He awoke the following morning, thinking he was dreaming it all, but when he got to his feet, his legs felt like jelly, and he succumbed to his own weight. He tried to stand a second time, but more slowly. He stamped his feet a couple of times and struggled to reach the other side of the tiny room.

Feeling more confident, he headed for the door, undid the latch, and walked into the sun-lit, cloistered yard outside. The monk was walking silently in the shade, his lips silently miming the ancient prayers that linked him to past and the future. He looked up when he saw Rosso, and going over to the boy, he directed him to the small refractory where he could break his fast.

The monk watched in silence as the boy ate bread and fruit, consuming with it a mug of watered wine. Wiping his face on his sleeve, Rosso looked up with a big grin. But what he saw sent ice into his soul. There were tears streaming down the face of that loving man.

"No!"

It seemed some disembodied soul had screamed that tiny word. Rosso, felt like he was observing the scene from some far away planet, was surprised that the voice he'd heard was his own. The screamed sound of his own voice returned him to the present. He leapt to his feet, sending the bench behind him tumbling.

"No, not Anna!" he shouted. "Please tell me she's okay. Please, Brother Damien, please tell me nothing has happened to my dear Anna. Please!"

Each time he said "please," the word lost conviction and seemed to wane. His heaving sobs grew louder until it seemed that his whole universe was full of grief and pain. When his wretched, abused, abandoned senses could take no more, he collapsed into the monk's arms and his mind faded again.

The sight of a crying child crying is heartbreaking, but what Damien saw was worse—a child numbed and isolated from all sense of reality due to cruelty and suffering. The monk appealed to the heavens for answers, but none appeared. For three days he felt helpless and hopeless as his young patient wandered in a place where none was able to reach him.

After three days, the priest led the lad outside for a walk. The sky was clear and the sun was low down in the western sky that was suffused with a glorious peach hue. The last rooks had left for their high perches in the woods and occasional swallows lingered to play low games with the early evening moths. The path led them to the cemetery, where little Anna had been laid to rest near her mother's grave. Rosso stared empty-faced at the marker, a single thought stirring in his mind. Why had they made such a big grave for such a small girl?

As he stared at the freshly turned earth, a straggling rook flew low overhead and let out a loud, "Caaw," causing Rosso and the monk glance up at the sky. in doing so, tears toweled in the boy's eyes as he crumpled to the ground, weeping atop the last mortal signs of his beloved sister. Looking up, he surprised the priest with a besmirched smile and sparkling eyes.

"He did it!" Rosso said almost laughing amongst his tears. "He did it."

Damien crouched, placing his hand on the young man's shoulder.

"Who did what, Rosso?" he asked, hoping the boy hadn't completely lost his mind.

"Anna asked if God would put a star in the heavens when she died," Rosso half-sobbed and half-smiled. "And look, *there* it is! It's the most beautiful star in the whole of the heavens."

He pointed toward the horizon, where the evening star shone alone in all its glory against a brilliant backdrop of pastel shades. The two hugged and laughed until the sky went dark, only to fill with a whole symphony of sparkling stars.

Rosso remained in the monastery for two additional days before returning to his house. He never referred to it as his "home" any longer, because all the love he had ever experienced there was gone. Father Damien spoke with him at the door before leaving.

"If you ever need me, Rosso—remember, I'll always be there for you. And wherever you go in the future, I'll pray for you every day of my life."

By that time, Rosso and Lorenzo were working the butcher's business alone. Lorenzo forced Rosso take on most of the menial duties, including lugging carcasses, cleaning up the blood and offal, sharpening the knives and carting the fetid remains to isolated marshy spots, where no one asked what was buried there. Their working arrangement would last as long as Rosso remained small and in fear of his brother, but the onset of adolescence was as irresistible as time itself. It wasn't long before Rosso reached adolescence, growing bigger, taller and stronger. His deepening voice cracked whilst speaking, causing Bastiano to tease him even more. But the scales of nature and justice began to balance.

One evening as Rosso was sharpening the knives, Bastiano approached in a particularly foul mood. He slammed the door, threw his empty bag on the floor and spat on it.

"The old man's *drunk* again, and he expects me to keep working so he can drink himself to death. What does he think I am? His bloody slave!"

Rosso chuckled at the sight of him, which only made Bastiano even more angry.

"You sniveling little wretch! You always were trouble!"

Picking up a cleaver, he made for Rosso.

Fear makes bold the timid. For Rosso, the approach of his brother with the cleaver, the memories of the abuse throughout his life and his grief at losing his beloved little sister came together to ignite a firestorm of rage. Grabbing the nearest knife, he threw himself on his brother who was overwhelmed by the unexpected onslaught.

Before Bastiano understood what was going on, he was flat on his back. and his red-faced, maniac younger brother was holding a very sharp knife across his throat, showering his own face with spittle.

"You will never say that to me again. Ever!"

In the silence that followed, there was only the sound of their breathing.

✜ ✜ ✜

Feeling at last vindicated, Rosso threw the knife to the ground, rose and left the cottage, slamming the door. He never returned.

3

ON THE ROAD

THE ENERGY OF Rosso's violent rage lasted all of five minutes. By the time his anger dissipated, he found himself on the desolate street in a damp drizzle of rain. Feeling alone and young, he knuckled a tear at the corner of his eye. He wiped his nose with the rags of his sleeve as he began to have second thoughts.

As he stood in the dark, trying to work out his next move, he caught sight of the small monastery, and without thinking, he walked towards it. Standing in front of the building, he summoned up the courage to knock in order to ask his friend Damien for help.

His nerve failed him, but his shivering body urged him to seek shelter. He crept around the back of the building and into the small shed that acted as a fowl house and home to three sheep and a tethered goat. The chickens bustled and cackled their displeasure at his appearance, whilst the sheep and goat stirred up the straw with their agitated footwork.

Rosso shushed them, made a bed out of the spare straw and settled down to sleep. If he dreamed that night, he didn't remember what. In the morning he, awoke refreshed and with a stubborn determination to never go back.

The foraging hens had awakened him early. They were pecking at something close by his head. Turning to see what it was, he realized that someone had placed a blanket over him during the night.

"Damien," he said, smiling to himself.

When he discovered the package of bread and cheese that the good monk left for him, he glanced in the direction of the monastery.

"Thank you, dear Damien."

He ate some of the bread, but he kept the remainder and the cheese for later. Folding the blanket, he placed it well out of the reach of the hungry goat that had been eying and nipping at it. Opening the shed door, he waved silent thanks in Domain's direction, turned his back on the village and left it forever.

Standing in the shadows of his cell, Brother Damien watched the boy leave, a heaviness and lightness competing in the good man's heart. In prayer, he sent battalions of imprecations to his Father in heaven, begging him to protect the lost young man as he went on his unknown journey. He remained motionless, looking out of his small window long after Rosso's slight figure finally disappeared.

Rosso had often traveled the half-hidden tracks while riding his father's carrion cart, and he knew their secrets well. He knew that his father had been involved in a business that should be plied on the open highways.

For the time being, Rosso chose the hidden paths, allowing him to get far from his village by the next day's break. Eventually, he broke through a gap in the hedge and joined those silent, shadowy figures who travelled slowly through the countryside, invisible in their cloaks of poverty.

He'd left with nothing but the shirt on his back, so he had little to lose. If he'd had shoes, then someone with no shoes would have been taken them from him, but he had no shoes. If he'd had a belt to secure his tattered trousers, then someone would have taken that too, but he had no belt. All he had was a scavenged piece of string to secure his cut-down canvas pants and enough food to last one day. That is why Rosso was left in peace to wander, alone and hungry, in a foreign place.

His hunger was often sated by the kindness of strangers who took pity on him as he passed. Perhaps they saw something in his face that reminded them of other children they had ignored who lived on in their consciences. Most it was the simple goodness of people who cherished life, who understood that they were giving not only food, but a moment of hope too.

Yet there were many dangers on the road as well.

Amongst those who moved unseen along the highways were some as lethal as venomous snakes. Simply to step into the shadow of such a creature's path could mean a sudden, silent death in some forgotten, lonely place. These assassins slithered through life, their bitter, cold hearts made of a stone that no sun could warm. They lay in wait for the weak and the vulnerable, and for such people as these, Rosso seemed a prime victim.

One day in the heat of the midday sun, a short distance outside a village where a kind lady had filled Rosso's stomach with the remnants of the family meal, a member of this hateful brood crept up behind him. He saw the creature's shadow before he heard the final footsteps. Instinct turned his head to catch a glimpse of the man. For a moment he froze, as the dusty features before him reminded him of Bastiano. And that, perhaps, saved his life.

The memory of his brother set every nerve in his body on edge as his eyes searched for a weapon. Yet upon closer inspection, Rosso realized that this grimy, disheveled, dishonest looking man was not his brother. He was stocky and threatening, like Bastiano, and wore a battered felt hat drawn down low over eyes that glittered beneath its sweat-soaked rim. Unlike his brother, there was a finger missing from the hand that repeatedly checked to see if its owner's earlobe was still in its correct position. His tongue flicked out between missing teeth, licking at his parched, cracked lips.

"Need a companion, young man," he said, checking again to see if his earlobe had moved.

"Don't need one," Rosso remarked, remaining where he was. "I'm heading off over *there* anyway."

He waved with his hand in no particular direction.

"Got any food or drink to share with a poor fellow traveler?" the man hissed, taking a step closer and becoming decidedly anxious about the position of his earlobe. Rosso held his ground, but he was certain the man could hear his racing heart, because it sounded like a drum in his own ears. The man's hand moved from his lobe to his hip.

"Haven't got anything," said Rosso, and flicking his eyes he saw a stone on the road behind the predator. The man saw his eyes move and snaked his head around to take a look.

When he thought about it later, Rosso couldn't remember why he decided to run for it, but he ran as fast and as far as he could along the road and then off into the country. His pursuer ran after him, but young lungs and a full stomach gave Rosso the edge he needed. After half a mile, the man slowed to a stop and yelled threats and obscenities at him, which were carried off by the breeze and sent into oblivion.

Rosso ran until his lungs were on fire and his legs sang for him to stop. He slowed his pace and looked back to where that once great threat was, which had become a distant speck, emasculated and impotent.

Looking around at the hilly landscape, Rosso decided that going forward, he would avoid the highway for a few days—in case his reptilian friend should try to follow him. Instead, he would find a path through the countryside to avoid the main road until he was certain he was safe.

Ahead on one of the small hills, there was a shepherd's hut, which he reached before lying down in the shade to have a rest. He didn't intend to fall asleep, but the warmth of the day and the relief of being far away from his attacker relaxed him. He felt his conscious mind, slipping loose.

He awoke to the sound of a cough and sat up, terrified, thinking his pursuer had tracked him down.

"Been aving a bad dream, son?" a friendly voice said, followed by the sound of laughter from another gruff throat. Rosso backed up to the wall of the hut, trying to shake the sleep from his eyes as he examined the man in front of him.

"Who are you?" he said, glancing from one face to the other, trying to gauge if either had evil intent.

"Bit of an inquisitor, eh?" said the lean man, whose stringy beard made a plain frame for a pair of animated eyes. "You're not one of the *Count's* men, are you?" he continued, assuming a stern face as he drew a sharp knife slowly from its sheath and began to clean his nails with it.

"Please, Sir—I'm not, Sir. I'm just a butcher's boy, who's run away from home and I've just been chased by a man who wanted to steal my food, cept I didn't have any food, so he couldn't, but he still chased me down the road, and so I had to come up here to hide."

The words having tumbled from his mind straight into his mouth stunned Rosso into silence.

The lean man rocked back and forth, roaring with laughter.

"Whoa there, lad! I was only *teasing* you."

He stopped to catch his breath.

"I reckon we've seen a few of the Count's men in our time, and we ain't never seen one dressed quite as fancy as *you* are!"

At this, his companion, a big youth with broad shoulders and a short cropped head, offered Rosso his hand and helped him to his feet.

Having regained his composure, the man with the stringy beard extended his hand.

"So you've taken to the road too, have you, lad? What's your name?"

"Rosso."

"Been on the road long"?

"No."

"Anyone going to *miss* you?"

Rosso paused, cautious. *Would* anyone miss him? He'd never had any friends, because he was never *allowed* to have any, apart from Anna, and she was dead. But there was Brother Damien, who had always been there for Rosso, who said he'd always pray for the lad.

"Perhaps," Rosso replied. "Perhaps there might be someone."

"Family?" asked stringy beard.

"No."

"Well this might be your lucky day then, young Rosso, cos we're always lookin for a young man who'd like to join our little family—a young man who might be keen to see the world and have a bit of an adventure too, eh?"

He turned to his friend, who smiled back, nodding.

"We're one big appy family ere, ain't we?"

Putting his arm around his companion's shoulder, he squeezed and they both looked toward Rosso.

"My name's Gino. We two companions ere travel the countryside, saving youths from falling into evil company," he said with a knowing grin, bowing. "So would you like to join us for the evening, young sir?"

Rosso's face cracked into a smile. It was the longest conversation he'd had for some time, and yet he felt strangely safe.

He bowed in return.

"I'd be delighted to, Gino. What's for supper?"

Hearing him, the two itinerants gave him several hearty slaps on the back whilst he blushed at his own bravado.

4
NEW FRIENDS, NEW ADVENTURES

GINO'S COMPANION was called Dominic, but apparently no one ever called him by that name.

"Gino always called me *The Dom*," he said. "It's different, but then we're all different, aren't we?"

He was the man who had helped Rosso to his feet, his close cropped skull surmounting a wide and welcoming face. Rosso liked him for the gentle expression in his eyes.

"Did you run away from home as well Dom?" he asked as they prepared to make camp for the night.

The genial giant looked down at his new friend.

"I suspect we've got a lot in common, young lad," he nodded, though he could not have been more than a couple of years older. "I've been with Gino for about two years now. There was another lad, but he upped and left last week, so it's good that we found you, cos now we're back up to full strength."

He spoke the last words with a disarming matter-of-fact-ness.

"Trouble is, he was the one who was real good at hunting for victuals. So you see, we're a bit short of hospitality, if you get my drift?"

Rosso shrugged.

"I might be able to help you there."

Dom stared at him for a moment before putting his arm around the boy's shoulder and shouting to Gino.

"I think we've got ourselves a new fetcha."

"What's a fetcha?" Rosso asked, looking up at the Dom.

"It's the bloke what fetches us our *food!*" Dom replied.

With a huge grin on his face, he gave his new friend a swift dig in the ribs, at which both laughed at his terrible joke.

The times that followed were the best of his short life so far. Rosso reveled in his new found friends and soon fell into their way of doing things. For Gino and his companions, plucking food from the countryside was seen as "fair game," and begging was a regular part of their itinerant life—but the act of stealing was a line they would not cross.

"Hunger can be a badge of honour and give a man dignity," Gino said to his friends. "Thievery can raise a man up slowly, but let him down quickly, at the end of a rope!"

On one summer day Gino, Rosso, and the Dom meandered up to a crossroads, around which an accretion of small dwellings had sprung up over the centuries, shaping itself into a small village over time. The first ambassadors to greet them from the languid metropolis were the usual assortment of mongrel dogs.

The younger ones barked wildly, whilst the older, more measured animals approached at a more thoughtful pace. These sniffed at the men's clothes, then having decided that they held no threat, retreated at a plodding pace to seek the shade somewhere to dream another canine dream.

Behind most of the small cottages were orchards of olive trees, now heavily laden with fruit. In front of one dwelling, standing apart, as if astonished at its isolation—was a goat, tethered to a post. As the men passed this caprine sentinel, it gave a mournful bleat.

A cheery-looking man immediately appeared at the cottage door, as if answering a knock. He shouted toward them.

"Are you lads looking for *work*? I need some help getting those olives off the trees before they all drop and rot. Are you up for a hard day's work?" he asked in a pleasant voice.

Gino looked at his friends and winked. Then turning, he walked up to the man.

"We never turn down an honest day's work, Sir."

He reached up to stroke his wispy beard.

"And tell me, master. What are the wages like hereabouts?"

"Jaw wages—as they say in our district. I'll feed you during the day, and then I'll give you more food for your journey, and a skin of the local wine too," he replied, patting Gino on the back. "How does that sound to you, my friend?"

Looking across at his companions, Gino gave them a nod, stroking his beard again.

"That sounds very fair to me, Sir. When do we start?"

"No time like the present," came the quick response.

With that Gino signaled for the three others to join him.

The men went around the back of the cottage, and just as they passed a small wooden shed, there came the sound of manic barking.

"My little darlings," the benevolent olive farmer smiled. "Docile as little lambs when they're out! They just want to come out and play with you. Perhaps later, eh?"

Moving to the orchard, he provided them the sheets, ladders, and baskets that they would need.

"I'll call down in a couple of hours with a cart to take the first load up to the store, and I'll bring some food down with me then," he said, his face suffused with an over-weaning smile.

Then he headed back to the cottage, leaving the young companions to their day of toil. They set off with great enthusiasm. It had been some weeks since they'd last had a job, and food always tasted so much better after working hard to earn the hunger!

Rosso picked one of the ripe fruit and squeezed it between his fingers. Thick white juice oozed from its bitter skin. It always seemed such a miracle to him that these acrid black fruit would produce such glorious golden oil. He picked up his long wand and swung it up into the branches. Hundreds more of the black berries fell into the welcoming blanket surrounding the gnarled, ancient trees.

True to his word, the man returned a couple of hours later with a cart, and he proceeded to load the overflowing baskets onto it. The only thing was—he didn't bring any food with him! When Gino asked him where the food was, the smiling man apologized and promised to go directly to the nearby town and get some fresh bread and meats. In the meantime, he'd leave them a stone jug, filled with watered wine, to help slake their thirst.

Perhaps they should have been even more suspicious after they'd tasted the watered wine. The Dom was the first to spit his on the ground, remarking "this tastes more like sweet vinegar"!

It began to dawn on the group that they were on the very horns of a dilemma: whether to believe the promise of good food to fill their growling stomachs from a man of dubious honesty, or to listen to the alarm bells clanging in their heads—and leave the rest of the fruit to rot, along with its owner!

After much head scratching, and at the desperate urgings from their hollow stomachs, they continued stripping the branches, gathering the berries that fell on the sheets and putting them into the remaining baskets.

When they finally heard the farmer's cart pull up to the front of the house, only a few trees remained to be stripped. On his way down to them, their merry host disappeared into the shed and reappeared with three black and vicious looking dogs that appeared to have an uncommon appetite for the young workers' flesh.

"Sorry lads," the benevolent farmer said with a malevolent grin on his chubby jowls. "They seem to be out of bread in town. Maybe you'll get more luck next time."

He let the leashes slip a little, allowing the black beasts to surge closer, their spittled mouths barking in the young men's faces. The farmer was barely able to restrain them from their ominous lunges.

"I don't believe this," the Dom cried in utter amazement at the betrayal. "We give you an honest day's work, and all you can do is cheat us out of a piece of bread?"

"That's why I'm fat and you're scrawny," their gloating oppressor shouted over the din of mad dogs. "And that' why I'm staying put and you're clearing out double smart before I get too tired and have to let go of these chains."

Slipping the frenzied demons' chains another few inches, the three hungry, furious workers were forced to retreat. They left for the road, wiping the dust from their garments as they left. Once they were at a safe distance, they looked back from the top of the hill and saw the man still standing there, holding his three black beasts and checking to make sure that the boys had truly left. Finally, he turned and went back into his house.

Gino was incandescent with rage and insistent on going back to burn down the house.

"That miserable, fat-faced wretch needs to be taught a lesson!"

"But you know what'd happen if we did anything like that, Gino," Dom said, trying to reason with his friend. "The whole neighbourhood would know in five minutes who'd done it, we'd be chased halfway across the countryside, and we'd still be no better off than we are now."

"You might be right there, Dom, but it sure don't make me feel any better," Gino glowered. "But setting light to his place would surely make me *feel* a whole lot better about it."

He picked up a stone and threw it as hard as he could in the direction of the house. It clattered along the road, stirring up a small cloud of dust before it was forgotten, along with his temper.

"I've got an idea," Rosso announced. "But it'd mean that we'd have to stick around until after he's headed back into the village with the rest of the load. How do you fancy a bit of fun and retribution?"

Gino and the Dom looked at each other with intrigued expressions.

"All depends," said the Dom, pausing. "What does retribution mean?"

"Don't worry, Dom. It's nothing terrible. In fact, you could look at it as us helping let nature take its course," he added, a wicked grin spreading across his innocent face. With that, they squatted down whilst he explained his plan.

There are two facts that all keepers of goats know well. First, goats can be intensely stubborn and difficult to shift, especially when they're eating, and second, they will eat anything and everything, twenty-four hours a day, given half the chance.

When the man had left for town with the baskets of olives, picked by the three men, presently starving, returned to the scene of the crime. There, the vengeful workers dragged the goat from the last remaining blades of grass within its tethered reach, and with much pulling and pushing, they managed to drag it into their ex-employers house.

Realizing that the farmer would take his time and predicting the goat would have a healthy appetite, they took the goat with them into the kitchen. They reasoned that what they consumed was fair reward for their hard day's work in the olive orchard. But by the way the goat ravenously consumed the tablecloths, the tattered curtains, two pairs of boots, and was feeding on a jacket, the lads surmised that he hadn't been fairly recompensed for his work for quite some considerable time either.

When the companions had eaten all they could, they thought that the goat still looked a little peckish. So leading it into the farmer's bedroom, they closed the door behind and left the building. They hardly had the strength to walk back down the lane. Such was the aching in their stomachs as they laughed about what they imagined would greet the farmer on his return, and the trials he would have trying to remove the goat and its excrement.

In time, the story about how the hungry goat had got into the farmer's house spread across the countryside. The cautionary tale did much to enhance the good reputation of Rosso and his friends, but it further blackened the reputation of the dishonest farmer, renowned for his devious and deceitful ways.

But just as there are those who thrive when planted in an environment of goodness, there are those who become blighted by malevolent influences. When those who are blighted meet those who have hope, then jealousy is born.

Some months later, the trio ventured to a large market town, renowned for its famous fair. The highlight of the week-long festival was a horse race around the piazza, with its stolen Egyptian obelisk standing like a sundial at its centre. Each of the local districts entered a horse and rider in the main event of the day.

But as well as racing, there was archery, acrobatics, dancing, food and wine! Walking up the long hill towards the town in the cool of the morning, each of the famished friends fantasied about the fantastic foods they'd eat at their own dream feast. Having salivated over their favorite imagined foods, their minds turned to women. They took turns describing the beauty, charms and scents of those lucky visions of womanhood who would have the honor of dancing with them around that famous obelisk.

Gino, the Dom and Rosso brushed off their dusty garments and straightened each other's attire as best as they could. The effect of a smile could light up even the shabbiest of suits. Therefore, from the broad grins on their faces as they entered the town, hearing the distant music, they ranked amongst the smartest people in the entire country.

Town life had its own colors. Smells and sounds were an intoxicating brew for those who were used to a rural life. Soon, they found themselves in the thickest of the crowd, squeezing between scented bodies, clothed in the softest of garments, along with sweatier bodies that were as much in need of repair as their own. Stalls groaned under the weight of freshly prepared foods.

They headed toward the music and stopped to admire those who were already weaving and twisting to the sound of the pipe and strings. There was a fine crowd gathered to watch the young ones dance. Rosso and his companions found a spot where they could scan the crowd and seek out suitable partners.

Rosso smelt her perfume before he saw her, and he was overcome by its seductive scent. He heard the rustle of her gown and felt the pressure of her thigh against his. Turning, he saw two walnut brown eyes, looking straight at him. She had the clearest of skin on her finely-set features, and her long black hair went flowed wildly across her face and down to her bare shoulders.

When she moved against him again, Rosso blushed at the intimate contact with an unknown woman. Coquettishly, she held his gaze.

"Are you afraid of me, boy?"

He tried to turn away, but she held onto his arm.

"How would you like to dance with a pretty girl then?"

Before he could answer, she took him by the hand and led him into the area where the other dancers spun. As she led, she sent a flashing look over his shoulder at something, or someone, beyond his vision.

For a young man, Rosso danced like a camel. Yet he was mesmerized, by his partner who moved her body seductively close to his body, all the while smiling at him. She was about to whisper something in his ear when someone spun him around.

A tall, handsome man stood before him, shouting, his face distorted by rage.

"Who said you could dance with my girl, vermin?"

His face calmed to an arrogant disdain. Before Rosso could answer, the man grabbed him by the hair and shouted to the encircling throng.

"We don't like vermin in our town, do we?"

He twisted Rosso's head toward the onlookers, who moments earlier were laughing with him, and were now deriding him.

"What do you think we should do with this vermin?" the arrogant man asked the crowd.

"I'd leave the poor chap *alone* if I were you!" a voice called from the rear of the assembled mass.

Like all fickle things, the crowd, once solid and densely packed, miraculously opened to reveal a bored-looking man of good features. He sat on a barrel, drinking a glass of wine.

"What did you say?" said he of the disdainful features. "How dare you speak to me like that! Perhaps you have a death wish?"

Pushing Rosso away, he made for the indolent one, who appeared at first to ignore him. He finished the glass of wine before wiping his mouth with his sleeve and looking playfully at the young man who towered over him.

"Do you know what?" he inquired, with the faintest trace of a French accent. "I think, perhaps, that you're a little too big for your boots."

He held up his hand to silence the youth, who was seething with rage.

"And that isn't all. I think you should *apologize* to that young fellow over there who has done you no harm whatsoever—apart from having the good sense to entertain that delightful young lady, who's obviously far too good for an ape like you."

Tilting his head, he poured himself another glass of wine.

Anger begets violence, which can cloud the senses and dull the mind. But arrogance can magnify both anger and violence, often with fatal consequences. Thinking his foe a fool and easy prey, Rosso's tormentor drew his dagger from its sheath, but the seemingly indolent youth was well prepared. He had hidden a stiletto under a cloth, just behind his jug of wine. In the moment his attacker leaned forward to thrust, he was mortally wounded by that vicious blade, which entered under his ribcage and reached into his foolish heart.

The aggressor seemed shocked as he stood there in the sudden silence of the crowd. Then he collapsed to the floor, as dead as the stones he fell on. There were muffled screams amongst the encircling crowd, but few had sympathy for the dead man. Yet if one were to pause and look at his face, frozen in death, with all the anger gone and without a trace of disdain, he would have been a beautiful young man at peace… at last.

5
COMINGS AND GOINGS

ROSSO APPROACHED as the victor was meticulously cleaning his blade with a cloth.

"How can I thank you?"

"Delighted to assist where I can," was the smooth reply "But I do find that fighting gives one an almost unquenchable thirst. Would you like to join me for a drink?"

He called for the servant to bring another jug of wine and extra glasses. Just then, the woman who had fanned the flames of passion that had led to the fight that ended in death, approached.

"He was always too pretty and too cocky for his own good," she said as his companions carried away his body. Lookin toward Rosso, she whispered.

"Choose your companions wisely young man."

Flashing a smile at the others, she swung around and disappeared into the crowd.

Jacques Villeprieux was French, but he spoke perfect Italian in the Roman dialect. He was charming and seemed to be at ease in his own person and with the world. The reason that Jacques Villeprieux was in that particular town at this particular time was just as much a mystery to him as it was to the three companions.

"But do not call me Jacques. Nobody calls me that, except for my mother. Everyone calls me Villeprieux," he explained to Rosso and the others..

He laughed when Rosso explained why he had been given his name, but he softened when he heard the young man's history.

"So, you're a butcher's son, eh?" he said pouring himself another glass "Myself, I've come across many butchers in this part of the world, my red-headed knife-sharpener, but not all of them are selling meat. *Bien sûr, mon ami*—it's all very well to sharpen knives to cut up dead meat, but can you use one in a fight?" he asked, seeming more interested in his new companion.

"I can skin a rabbit and gut a sheep or a beast, but I've never used a blade on a man, if that's what you mean," Rosso replied "I always sharpened the boning knives back home, and I had to do a good job, or else."

For a moment, he could see his father before him, his face red with rage—should the edge on a blade not be to his liking. Rosso shook his head as if to clear the image from his mind.

"And what about you, big fellow?" asked Villeprieux, turning to the Dom. "I'd wager that you'd be a fine fellow to have on my side if it came to a decent brawl."

The Dom shrugged his shoulders.

"I've never seen the value in getting into a fight, really. But if my friends were in trouble, I wouldn't let any harm come to em."

As he spoke, the Dom endowed his words with an air of dignity.

"So would a *dog*," Villeprieux concluded.

Though the comment was made in a light hearted manner, something in Gino grimaced at the tone in which it was said.

But Rosso saw only goodness in his benefactor. He asked in innocence about where in France Villeprieux had grown up and where he'd been since. Villeprieux answered with a disinterested vagueness, as if he were speaking about someone else. He recounted that his family had "property" in France, "somewhere" near Paris. His father was dead. "The pox, I believe," he said.

That stark statement was the only time he ever mentioned his father. His mother brought him up as an only child.

"I suspect that she spoiled me and made me prone to bouts of boredom," and that was all he cared to say of his mother. He had left home "sometime ago," because of "some misunderstanding," but the details were lost to them as he proceeded to indulged in a theatrical stretch and an all-encompassing yawn. After that, he was a bit vague about everything."

Reverting to his previous good form, he delighted them with stories of France and of Rome, where he had spent some years, "just wandering about."

Both the Dom and Rosso were enchanted by Ville-prieux. For Gino however, there was something about their new companion that made him keep his distance. As the evening wore on, and Villepreiux asked where they were going next, Gino answered.

"We're heading for Florence to see the tourney there."

"From the rumors I hear, there'll be more than a tourney in Florence in the not too distant future."

Draining his goblet, he slammed it down on the table and wiped his mouth. Standing, he appealed to the others.

"*Mes amis*, I've seen just about all I need to of this dread-ful, dull little town, and it may be that the friends of the recently deceased might not hold me in the highest esteem. So may I propose that I join you on your travels?"

He turned to Rosso, tousling his already unruly hair.

"And as my friend here seems to attract the best-look-ing whores, it seems that you'll need all the help you can to keep him out of trouble."

Rosso blushed.

All relationships are unique, but often what we see reflected in friendships is a glimpse of some facet of our own per-sonalities. Perhaps that was why Rosso thought Ville-prieux to be full of goodness, of high nobility and the best of intentions. The Dom saw him as fearless, brave and loyal, while Gino wondered what exactly it was that he saw in the Frenchman.

In the seasons ahead, as Gino became more used to the moods of his new companion, he learned to respect him more, although he still held a small part of himself separate from the charms of their beguiling Gallic confrere. They weaved their ways through the towns and surrounding countryside, working where and when they could. But like all free young men, they still had not quite escaped the impishness of youth.

A certain Parish priest hunted them from his village, accusing them of being sinful vagabonds. The very next day, the priest was staggered to find that his undergarments were proudly displayed on a long line outside of the rectory, interspersed with similar garments normally worn by the more colorful ladies of the district. To compound his embarrassment, it happened to be market day, and being a small village, no one missed the entertaining display.

During the next few months, the priest gave sermons that were remarkable for their brevity and humility. Whilst he may have slipped in the estimation of the ladies of that village, paradoxically, he was greeted far more warmly than he would have liked by the males of the village.

One day. Villeprieux took it into his head to make an improvement in Rosso's education, deciding to teach him French.

"It's the language of the elite, of the educated and the language of the true gentleman," he proclaimed one day.

"So this is what I propose, my red-headed one: every night, you will tell me whatever story you like, and I shall translate it into French. Then I shall teach you to say it back to me. *Certainment*, it will be intolerably dull at first, but you are quick, and I' am an excellent teacher. It is certain that you will pick it up in no time at all. After all, your teacher will be the best French teacher this country can provide."

He paused as he looked about the countryside.

"After all, what else is there to do in this country of peasants?"

So the pact was made. When there was food to be had, they made a small feast of it and followed with storytelling and translating. When there was no food to be had, the evenings were longer, the stomachs noisier, and Rosso found that Villepreiux struggled against dark moods that seemed to be clawing to escape him. Rosso admired Villepreiux even more for the effort he made against his inner turmoil, and he was determined to try his best to be a good student.

Their long slow journey towards Florence came to an end, with Rosso was nearly word-perfect in his French, conversing freely with Villepreiux in his native tongue.

"I *know* this area!" Gino declared one day. "See that farm over there—that farm was once owned by some friends of mine."

They all looked across the valley to where a low stone building seemed to grow out of the hillside. All around it, the land was lush and fertile, dotted with the white pelts of grazing sheep. Behind the house was a small copse of Olive trees.

"And that hut up on the hill opposite—that's the shepherd's hut where my Dad taught me all about tending sheep."

The memories of those distant days played vividly in his mind.

"He doesn't look like much of a shepherd to me. His beard is too—how do you say, *threadbare*?" Villeprieux countered, yawning.

"Why did you leave?" Rosso asked, ignoring his colleague. Gino stood.

"Good question, really."

He paused as he did when deciding which path he should follow.

"Why did I leave? See that farmhouse over there that I pointed out earlier? When I was a little boy growing up, I lived in that house with the farmer's family in the summer when my Dad was out with his flock. My best friend lived there, and she was the same age as me. We played all around the old house, in that barn behind the house, and up in them fields where the olives are growing."

He paused again.

"Her name was Maria, and she was the beautiful little friend that I always thought I would marry. But, well, that's life, eh."

Villeprieux attempted to look bored, but he failed.,
"So?"

"My Mum died giving birth to me, so I was all my Dad ever had. He was a good man, and the one thing he kept on hammering into my thick skull was, 'Always tell the truth son, cos it's truth what really makes you free,' which for a young lad was difficult to digest. Or sometimes he'd say, 'Gino, my lad, honesty ain't the best policy. It's the only policy.'"

He stopped to pluck a long stem of grass and chewed on it, as if reliving each moment he was recounting.

"Some ruffians came to him one day and threatened to kill him if he didn't give them a sheep to kill and eat. My Dad said it was impossible, cos the owner knew how many sheep there were and he had to account for them all. Well, those ruffians kept their word. I found my Dad the next day, covered in the guts of the sheep that they'd slaughtered. They'd cut his tongue out and nailed it to the wall of the hut. That tongue had never uttered a dishonest word, and they hated him for it. That's why they cut it out."

The Dom, Rosso, and Villeprieux maintained their silence whilst Gino clenched his jaw, remembering each detail.

"I buried him behind the hut—right where he'd always been, on the side of the hill, with his beloved sheep and the open sky above him. Then I suppose things had to change. I was too small to take on being a shepherd. A new man arrived, and I wasn't wanted any more. Not that the farmer kicked me out—my little Maria wouldn't have that, cos her little heart loved me just as much as I loved her. I had to go, but I promised I'd come back. That was such a long time ago that she's probably married by now."

"Well let's find out, you sheep-headed imbecile," exclaimed Villeprieux, who started off down the hill towards the farmhouse.

"Now don't let's get too hasty here," said Gino running down after him. "She probably won't remember me, anyway."

"Not if she has any sense," smiled the Frenchman, striding towards the ever-nearing house whilst Rosso and the Dom followed behind with big grins on their faces.

Villeprieux stopped at the door, straightened his jacket and gave three quick raps on the wooden door. Gino whispered in the silence.

"I don't think there's anyone home, so perhaps we should just slip away quietly."

When the door opened, a young working woman stepped out of the shadow, brushing away a stray strand of hair had fallen across her face.. The rest of her hair was held back in a triangular scarf that matched the apron around her waist. She was of medium stature, bordering on a little stout. Her face was that of a good and gentle person, whilst her calloused hands belied years of cutting and chopping, of the cold frosts and the harsh scrubbing they had experienced since childhood.

"How may I help you?" she asked, looking first at Villeprieux and then at the others.

Gino had held back but finally her eyes settled on him. Her hand went to her mouth as a tear appeared on her cheek.

"Is that really *you*, Gino," she whispered. "Could it really be you, after all these years?"

Her whole body trembled as she spoke.

"I'm sorry to report, Madam, that it is Gino," the Frenchman answered, with a touch of sarcasm in his voice.

"It's me, Maria," said Gino, stepping forward to see her.

They stood looking at one another for what seemed like a long time, despite the other men shuffling from one foot to another.

"Why don't we come back in a little while—when you've finished talking?" Rosso suggested as he pushed the other two back.

"We'll be back once we've had a rest, Gino. Just give a whistle if you need us."

With that, they left, though neither Maria nor Gino had heard a single word.

They talked in a stuttering fashion at first, but soon the torrent of happiness washed away their walled-up dams of reserve. Soon, they were at that point where they had parted as children, but this time, the foundation of childish intimacy was layered with a tender, enduring love. A voice from within the farmhouse interrupted them.

"That's Papa, Maria said, blushing. "You remember him, don't you?"

"Of course I do. How could I forget him? He was like a second father to me when Dad died."

"The years haven't been kind to him, Gino. He's failed a lot now."

With a sadness in her voice, she whispered.

"It's his heart, I think. He can't do the things he used to do and that can make him a little short sometimes. But otherwise, he's the same dear Papa to me. And I don't mind the extra work. I'm still young, after all."

Giving Gino a cheeky grin, she turned and went inside.

"I'm coming, Papa, and I've got a surprise for you!"

Some hours later, Gino wandered down the farm track to find his friends.

"Maria would like you to join us for a meal," he muttered, scuffing the dust with the toe of his boot.

"*What's* this?" said Villeprieux his eyebrows shooting up, "Join *us* for a meal?"

He looked at the Dom, giving him a theatrical wink, and he followed by bowing to Gino.

"Well, Monsieur, your humble servants would count it an honor to join you and the delightful Madmoiselle Maria for a meal."

"Sarcasm becomes you, Villeprieux," Gino groaned, blushing as red as the hair on Rosso's head. Turning on his heel in a vain attempt to avoid further barbs, Gino led them back down the track.

The little farmhouse was plain and simple, but it was warm and welcoming. Gino let them in through the low wooden door. The dry, earthen floor had been packed hard by generations of feet and shone with the brushings Maria gave it each day. The old farmer sat on his stool in the corner of the fireplace.

Each of the men removed his head covering and paid their respect to the aged man while glancing around the little homely room. The fire crackled, its dancing flames sending out eddies of warmth and light. A scent of soup in the air set their salivary glands to work in earnest anticipation of welcoming it into their empty stomachs.

"I hope you're hungry," Maria said as she entered the room with the large tureen. Yet before they could answer, she shooed them to the ready-laden table. Soon, they were tucking into their food and swapping stories of adventure, troubled times and hopes for a glorious future.

The old man joined them at the head of the table, his white head nodding as he listened and his dark eyes sparkling at the sight of his daughter beaming toward her long lost friend. The Dom was seated next to the old man.

"How do you manage this place all by yourself, Master?" he asked.

"I couldn't do it without her," he said, pointing toward Maria with his knife.

"She's the pillar of strength in this house. I'm afraid I can't do as much as I'd like anymore. And now with harvest here, there's a stack of work to be done."

The big-hearted Dom turned toward his companions.

"I don't think we've got any appointments for next week, do we, gentlemen? And this seems like a nice spot to settle into for a week or two, eh? From what I hear, from my good friend, Gino, the victuals and accommodation are excellent, so why don't we stay here for a couple of weeks. That way, maybe we could give this good farmer a hand with getting his harvest in—unless, of course, Monsewer Villeprieux needs to visit his tailor to get measured for a new suit for when he visits his Lordships in Florence."

They all laughed at the uncommon long speech from the young giant. Villeprieux's laughter was the loudest, even though it was at his own expense.

"Well said, young man. It is just what we need after our idling on the highways and byways. *Bien sûr*, a bit of hard work and some decent food will do us all some good. What do you say, Gino? Or perhaps I should defer to the beautiful lady of the house?"

Gino, who had become habitually red in the face, could only mumble.

"Sounds alright to me, I s'ppose."

Without thinking, Maria reached out and grasped his hand. This slight movement elicited more whoops of joy and fun from his friends, and the gesture succeeded in adding a throbbing sensation to the ruddy glow of the poor man's expression.

Theirs was a family farm, similar to others in the region. It had been a family farm for generations. As such, it had endured all the vicissitudes that nature and time provided. The graves of their forebearers, in a nearby field, stood like stone pages, recounting the instructions that nature attempted to instill in them down long, dark years.

Franco, dead, 28, fever, in God's care. Maria, dead, 19, childbirth, in God's care. Marco, dead, 78, dropsy, in God's care. Franco, dead, 36, accident, in God's care. Some pages were indecipherable and rested in the grass, looking up at the deep blue sky. Others were overgrown with weeds and seeded with saplings. The most recent pages had been cleared and were well-tended. Around them, the grass was trampled flat where Maria's feet and knees had been whilst she unburdened her soul to the spirit of her mother, now in

God's care. *Nature and nurture—perhaps it knows no boundaries*, Rosso thought as he passed that sacred place one day.

The farm had sheep that needed shearing. Shearers need clippers that needed to be sharp. Rosso knew how to sharpen them, and therefore Rosso would shear the sheep. This had been the irresistible logic of Villeprieux earlier that morning, and for that reason, he was on his way to bring some sheep down from the pasture to have them sheared. Gino had volunteered to go with him, along with the farm dog that danced around his legs in a skittish attempt to make Gino throw a stick

"That dog acts like it's your master," Rosso joked.

"Shouldn't that be the other way around?" Gino retorted.

"*Non*," the Frenchman replied. "I think he's trained you pretty well in the last few days!"

Both laughed at the truth of the statement.

"Rosso," Gino whispered after a pause. "I've got something to tell you, and I wanted you to be the first one I told."

The breeze ruffled the dry grass in the distance.

"You're *staying* here aren't you?" Rosso asked.

"How did you know?" a confused looking Gino stuttered.

"Because you and Maria love each other, and it's natural that you'd want to stay here with her and get married. I may have red hair, but I don't have the brain of a carrot, you know."

Throwing his arms around his dearest companion, they hugged

"Of course we'll all miss you," he continued. "And we'll all probably end up in prison without you to keep us honest. But you've been a better friend to me than any man could be. I was a scared, wounded, angry, ignorant brat, and yet you've been so tolerant and patient with me."

He paused in contemplation and continued.

"And it was you who taught me the meaning of forgiveness. You'll always be the best brother I ever had."

As they embraced again, Rosso felt the small muscles in his neck tighten with emotion. He swallowed hard. Wiping his face on his sleeve, Gino smiled.

"Who said you weren't *still* an ignorant brat?"

Giving Rosso a push, he ran off, with Rosso in hot pursuit—not quite sure whether he should be really happy or really sad.

Soon, all the farm winter preparation was done, and it was time for the companions to say their final farewell. They had their last meal together in the homely house. The farmer, with his white hair, nodded at all their tall tales, but he couldn't conceal his pride for Maria and Gino, soon to be betrothed

"I've been doubly blessed," he said during a lull in the banter. "I ave the best daughter a man could ave, and now I've got the best son a man could ave. If that ain't being doubly blessed, then I don't know what is."

No one at that table could disagree with him.

The next morning, Rosso, the Dom and Villeprieux prepared to leave. Maria squeezed food into the last small spots into Rosso's pack, which she then adjusted on his shoulders.

"Thank you for being such a good friend for Gino all these years. I never stopped loving him, you know, and there was never anyone else in this world for me. Now he's back."

Brushing an imaginary fleck from his shoulder, she continued.

"And I hope you won't mind me saying this to you, Gino's best of friends, but be mindful of yourself especially where Monsieur Villeprieux is concerned. It may be just a poor simple farm girl's intuition, but that one's different from the rest of you. Gino says so too. Just be careful is all I ask."

"Dearest of dear women," said Rosso in reply, "Of *course* he's different—he's French," he laughed to deflect her concerns. "And you keep an eye on Gino, because *he's* different too. He has the most generous heart that ever did beat in a man's chest, and I shall treasure his friendship until the end of my days."

She kissed him on the cheek upon hearing him say those words, turning away to hide the tears of happiness on her pretty red face.

The travelers hugged Gino in turn. They gave Maria a kiss on each cheek, along with various silly suggestions on how best to control her soon-to-be husband, Finally, they shook hands with the farmer who was seated in his chair by the fire, and then they walked off down the road, pausing at the bend to wave back at the diminishing figures who were embracing each other at the farm's front door.

"Well, *mes amis*," Villeprieux announced. "I feel a new adventure coming on."

"It's strange," the Dom replied, "I didn't want the *last* one to end. But it did, and it had a happy ending for Gino, and that makes me happy too."

After a pause, he continued.

"But you know what? It's left me feeling a little bit too—like when you've been at the best fair ever, but now it's over and you've gotta leave."

Sighing, he looked over at Rosso.

"I wonder where the road will lead us now?"

But within the next few paces, the road had gathered them into its bosom, leaving them to reflect on things, light and dark, from the past, and the hope and doubt of the future.

6

WALKING TO WAR

A GROUP OF three can quickly become a group of two—unless one of its members has a gentle soul. The Dom was that gentle soul. From the moment he pulled Rosso to his feet when they'd met at the shepherd's hut, he'd been the kind of brother that Rosso dreamed of having in those shadowed days of his early life.

The Dom was a gentle influence, gifted with the ability to stay serene when others laughed at him. He even seemed unperturbed when Villeprieux referred to him as "my oxen friend." All these gentle acts of humility seeped into the wounds of Rosso's childhood memories, silently helping to heal them.

So the trio trudged on together and for the next few months, meandering across Italy, making do and making fun whenever and wherever they went By the time they reached Florence, they heard rumors about a rift between the Romans and the Florentines. There were whispers about a Spanish invasion, which had the Florentines on edge, because an invasion meant war!

Wandering along, whenever they entered a town, Villeprieux headed for the tavern to glean news, and he would be silent and withdrawn for long periods upon his return. When the Dom asked what questioned him about what he heard, the reply would always be the same.

"Nothing to worry your dear dense dome with, *mon petit*. You just leave the thinking to me."

At that, the Dom would shrug and sit in silence, immersing himself in his surroundings. They were staying in a lean-to shed, where they'd found work during the grape picking season. The summer had been a long one, lingering well into autumn.

One night when Villeprieux was still at the tavern, as Rosso leaned against the shed, watching the fireflies whilst sharpening his knife, the Dom sat next to him.

"Do *you* think I'm stupid?" he asked.

Rosso set down his whetstone, cleaned the shining blade on his sleeve and glanced at his friend.

"I've never known a kinder, more thoughtful man than you, Dom. And I doubt I ever will."

"But do you think I'm *stupid*, because Villeprieux thinks I'm a simpleton?" he persisted.

"Sometimes, I think that Villeprieux has trouble translating his meaning from French into English," Rosso answered, irritated that he should have to defend his hero.

Taking a deep breath, Rosso calmed his mind, while the Dom serenely contemplated the stars.

"Dom," Rosso said, breaking the silence. "Villeprieux has a fast mind that works differently to most people. He enjoys excitement and finds things that we might call quiet times as difficult to endure—they make him listless and unsettled. But as for you being stupid, the answer is a very definite *no*. In my book, it takes a deal of wisdom to be content in your own company."

The Dom had been watching him all the time whilst he spoke. The gentleness of the large man's features seemed to take form, reaching out and with an invisible hand to touch Rosso's heart.

"Thank you, my friend."

Those were his final words on the subject. It was never raised again.

Villeprieux was up early the next day, a little the worse for wear and prepared to head back to town.

"I need to talk to some people," was all he said.

"How can he afford to stay in a tavern all night and pay for his drink?" the Dom asked, scratching the top of his cropped head.

"I suspect that, as well as being the charming rogue that we know him to be, one of his other gifts is being a successful gambler," Rosso answered, suppressing a smile.

Villeprieux tried to teach his young protégé the finer skills of cards and dice, but his bewildered pupil never caught on. Besides, Villeprieux's habit of taking Rosso's money did not provide the best incentive to continue.

"But I wonder what he's up to *this* time?" Rosso wondered.

They didn't have to wait long, as the Frenchman returned within the hour in the company of a very strange companion. The man rode a small Jennet, and yet his feet hardly reached the short stirrups. He wore a battered hat on his massive head, all the while waving his arms at Villeprieux in animated conversation.

Dismounting from his horse, the Frenchman introduced his stumpy companion.

"*Mes amis*, meet an old friend and counselor—Monsieur Oddysseo!"

Upon being introduced, the small man almost fell from his Jennet, picked up his hat from the road, punched it back into shape and planted it back on his head.

The Dom and Rosso looked at the man and back to each other, torn between amazement and embarrassment.

"I see you haven't had the pleasure of meeting a *dwarf* before?" Oddysseo asked as he climbed onto a table to look them both straight in their eyes. Removing his hat and giving it another punch to keep their attention, he went on.

"A shut mouth catches no flies." he leered at them.

They snapped their mouths shut in unison.

"As I was saying, you'll find that my noggin is exactly the same size as the turnips on top of your necks. It's just that you, gentlemen, have been cursed with having over-sized arms and legs. Sadly, that dis-articulated logic allows most of you to think that most of us are either children, or stupid, or both."

Replacing his hat, he continued.

"But I'd pit my brain against any of yours, including our French friend here, any day."

His expression dared a challenge.

"Such a performer," Villeprieux yawned. "Perhaps that's why he's in the circus! But his talents are lost there. He has brought me some news. There's to be a war, and the money's on the Spanish to teach our Florentine friends a lesson. These Spanish have a lot of gold to pay for mercenaries. Without a doubt, you've heard of the treasures they've brought back from the Americas."

"Whoa! Hold on there," said the Dom, "What's this about war, and what's this about mercenaries?"

"Ah," Villeprieux mused. "The Florentines have made the bad mistake of upsetting the Pope in Rome. And of course, that saintly man has asked his good friends in Spain to help him out. It just so happens that my good friend here, Oddysseo, got hold of this news and has kindly informed me about it. He also just happened to mention that the Florentines haven't taken kindly to the idea that the Spanish want to take over their castles, their lands, and especially, their women. So, my friends, I've taken the liberty of signing us all up with the Florentine army to help defend themselves against these accursed Spanish. And to prove their gratitude and affection, here's a bag of gold the Florentines have given me in return for our services."

He pulled a bag from his belt, and as he dropped it onto a pewter plate, out rolled gleaming golden florins.

Rosso and the Dom were speechless.

"We're not fighters," the Dom protested with a look of desperation and confusion.

"Calm yourself, my friends. Be patient and listen to what I have to say," Villeprieux answered. "It was a simple commercial decision, and anyway—the prospects aren't as bleak as most would think for our friends, the Florentines. And don't worry, dear Rosso—I didn't sign you up to *fight*."

He paused, smiling slyly at Oddysseo, who had now sat on the table, eating a crust of bread.

"Your talents will be better occupied working in the armory, keeping all the weapons sharp and ready for battle."

He turned toward the Dom.

"And don't worry, my gentle giant. Wars are a little different in this part of the world. Most of the time, it's all worked out before any battles are fought—some money is paid here, someone loses his land there, both sides sign a new treaty, and then, everyone goes home without anyone getting hurt."

"But from *my* experience," Oddysseo interrupted, spattering a few dry crumbs from his mouth as he spoke. "Whenever mon-sewer Villprieux is involved in any of these negotiations, it always happens that a great deal of the gold ends up in *his* purse too."

After swallowing his crust, he added, "And when was the last time you ended up on the losing side, even if it lost?"

"In the meantime, brave and gentle giant," continued Villeprieux, ignoring the dwarf. "You'll be one of the best foot soldiers the Florentines will have ever seen. I'll make it my personal duty to train you how to use a sword, a spear and a shield. You'll be my personal bodyguard and will be at my side at all times to protect me, because naturally, the Florentines have asked me to lead one of their bands."

Oddysseo paused from devouring the final piece of his crust, giving Villeprieux a curious look.

"There's an awful lot to think about here," said Rosso. "I'm not sure if I want to *go* to any wars—even if it's just to sharpen the swords and knives."

"I'm sorry, my friend," said Villeprieux, "But you have little choice—now that we have the Florentine gold. I don't think that they'd be very happy if we took their gold and didn't fight."

"So why don't we just give it back?" Rosso suggested.

"I think that it's a little too late for that now," said the Frenchman, shrugging his shoulders. "I gave them my word."

"And believe me," said Oddysseo, "That's a very expensive commodity in the current climate."

The Dom or Rosso had far less time than they would have preferred to consider what Villeprieux had done. That very afternoon, he led them back into the town to pick up supplies, bidding farewell to Oddysseo, who was moving on with the circus.

The little man remained on his Jennet as he bid them goodbye, giving his hat its ritual beating back-into-shape as he whispered to Rosso.

"He's not all he appears to be."

Yet before Rosso could reply, the dwarf gave the Jennet a mighty kick in the side. The ass moved down the road at a furious pace, braying loudly. As little man and big beast disappeared in a cloud of dust, they could still hear the dwarf roaring back at the irate jennet.

"What a strange little man," Rosso said to Villeprieux. "Angry, and yet kind. A clown, and yet wise! He's my kind of person."

"All such as he are strange," Villeprieux groaned with his typical disdain. "But he has proved to be a useful informer for me over the years."

For the next few days, he led his two companions to the other side of the town and into the countryside to meet up with the Florentines. He spent much of the extra time instructing the Dom in simple arms training. For a big man, the Dom moved quickly on his feet, and possessed a natural balance and fast reflexes.

"You were *made* for fighting," his new leader praised.

"I know," the Dom nodded. "But I don't have to like it, do I?"

Later on, when they were alone together, the big man spoke with Rosso.

"Have you ever *killed* someone?"

"Never. But I came close once, and I didn't like the way it felt."

Shuddering, he recalled how he'd nearly slit his own brother's throat.

"*I* killed someone once," the Dom volunteered. "He was trying to do terrible things to my sister. I crushed his head with a rock. It was such an awful sound and a horrible sight!"

All that could be heard in the ensuing silence was the swaying of the dry meadow grass, disturbed by a spirited breezed.

"To make matters worse, he was the local Duke's bastard son, and the local Duke was none too happy about it. And my sister—she had to leave too, because otherwise she'd have ended up dead as well."

He fell silent, remembering.

"I never saw my sister again after that."

The breeze settled as far away, a hawk hovered over the hillside.

"Killing people has dreadful consequences for everyone, I reckon," he continued, listlessly. "And it don't get much easier with time either.

"I'll fight if I have to," the Dom concluded, emerging from his torpor, "because it's important to look after your friends. Villeprieux has always done his best to look after me, so it's only right that I do my best to take care of him."

Rosso was less sure. He loved Villeprieux, and he loved the Dom too, but there was imbalance in the equation between the two of them.

Villeprieux's rag tag band of mercenaries was made up of vagrant youth, but rounded out by battle-hardened fighters from England and Scotland, along with several powerful swordsmen from the Holy Roman Empire. There were even a few French mercenaries, who delighted that their leader was from their own land, and they were the most vocal of all the band. Rosso was happy with the new company too.

"Well, there's a sight for sore eyes," he said one day to the Dom. "See that Scot over there? He's another carrot top! At last, I won't be the only one in town with red hair."

The Dom looked at the Scot with his wild red mop of tangled hair and thick freckled white arms and smiled.

"It's strange the things that make us happy."

Putting his arms around Rosso, he gave him a playful hug.

"Put me down, you black-haired brute," Rosso cried through his laughter. "And pick on someone your own size—like a small mountain or something!"

After some playful roughhousing, the Dom let Rosso go. "Let's get some food. I'm hungry."

They walked off arm in arm—two happy people who were oblivious about what would happen next.

Although it was a disparate group, there was a common purpose: to go into battle and to win. Winning mostly meant staying alive, with the added bonus of perhaps enough booty after the battle to buy a small patch of land. That was the lure for most men, but for others it had become a way of life.

Those steely-eyed killers had lost their sense of humanity. They'd lived in too many camps, gotten drunk in too many taverns and killed too many people to remember what kindness was. For all intents and purposes, they were immensely powerful men, but their souls had withered to dust. War had a way eviscerating the hearts of those who survived

Winning was a different thing for their captains and their kings. For those men, whose silken robes rarely felt sweat unless the sun shone too hotly on their remote positions, winning meant more riches and more power. Not surprising, Villeprieux proved to be a very effective commander.

"I didn't know you could speak English," Rosso mentioned one morning after battle practice.

"It's nothing," the Frenchman replied, as if avoiding the subject.

"Where did you learn it," persisted his earnest friend.

"Oh, I think that perhaps Maman employed some tutor who spoke that language. It's not difficult to pick it up, I think."

His eyes returned to the map he was viewing.

"My dear friend, Villeprieux, you never cease to amaze me!" Rosso said, shaking his head at another of the Frenchmen's seemingly natural gifts.

Villeprieux turned to look Rosso straight in the eye, and he responded in a voice that was full of quiet indulgence.

"My dear friend, you're too earnest in your affections. Believe me, I don't deserve them. One day, I may be as good a man as you are, but I doubt it. At heart, I'm a feckless wretch and you shouldn't trust me."

Rosso looked back into those jet black eyes, searching for the humor, but he found none. At last, he broke the spell, laughing.

"Villeprieux! Well, that must make you the greatest scoundrel that the world has ever seen! Just wait till I tell everyone what sort of comedian is leading them to victory."

Both laughed half-heartedly at the statement.

As the days turned into weeks, the group became closer, and despite the language differences, they understood each other perfectly. Each one disciplined himself, while Villeprieux disciplined them all. They were spoiling for a fight and would comport themselves well. The Spanish had arrived in force and were moving in from the west coast toward Florence. Villeprieux's group was involved in some minor skirmishes as each side tested each other's resources while maintaining distance from each other.

7

DEATH AND RESURRECTION

IT WAS STILL dark when Rosso stirred from his dream-filled sleep. The dawn invaded the starry skies from its unseen horizon, bringing light that gave color to the things it touched and voices to the things that flew. A few proud sentinel stars lingered to remind observers of the heavenly jewels that guide men through the inkiness of night.

Nearby, dark trees began to stir, their troubled black boughs disturbed by the message born by the daybreak breeze. There was a slight rime on the grass, but the misty early morning light suggested it was going to be a hot day. Rosso knew what he had to do and proceeded to the grinding stones whilst tightening his belt and grubbing in his pocket for some bread to give him strength.

He thought it strange that his childhood misery, involving sharpening knives so that his father and brother could slit

the throats of animals, had brought him such a fate. Iron-
ically, the knives he currently sharpened would be used to
slit the throats of men.

*True, that's if you could call these invading Spanish merce-
naries men*, he thought to himself. It then struck him that
he was a mercenary too, and a Venetian one at that! Rele-
gating those thoughts to the back of his mind, he reminded
himself that he had a job to do, and he knew he was good at
it. Villeprieux often told Rosso that he was the best recruit
ever. In Rosso's eyes, there was no greater compliment.

"Blunt knives will not dispatch your enemy swiftly," his
friend would say. "And that is not good for a soldier. *Bien
sûr*, if you leave an enemy badly wounded but very angry
with you, it is you that might end up getting killed! *Mes
amis*, it is our duty to dispatch our enemies with honour.
Wounds from blunted blades lead to pus and maggots. A
slow lingering death in some rat-infested shed, filled with
the stench of puss and foul humors, is not the glorious end
we soldiers deserve!"

Clapping his young friend around the shoulders, he
smiled.

"Give me one of Monsieur Rosso's razor-sharp blades any
day, and then I'll dispatch my enemy with dignity and send
him speedily to meet his Maker."

Smiling as he recalled Villeprieux's face, with its reck-
less good looks and long blond hair, Rosso cinched his belt
hard and checked his sharpening tools. As the sun began
to warm the air for the next few hours, he was busy putting
keen edges on a plethora of blades. Differing blades needed
different skills to hone them to perfection. Big broadswords

and axes needed the wheel, whilst the daggers and lancets needed a gentler hand, but Rosso knew his steel, and all the blades that went through his hands were sure to sing a true song when the fight finally came.

The mood in the camp was relaxed, as most of his comrades were certain that the rival leaders would reach an agreement before the sun reached its zenith. Hopefully, there would be no need to meet on the battlefield. For the past three mornings, Villeprieux himself had ridden off alone to parlay with the Spanish mercenaries, and he always returned, bearing reassuring news that all would be well.

That very morning, he set out for a fourth time to parlay, whilst his men went through their daily drills of training in a relaxed manner. It was a strange but usual fact that in most of the skirmishes between these Ducal States, the mercenaries on both sides often knew each other quite well, having drunk together, and in some cases, even fought together on the same side in previous campaigns. But this time, the Spanish had come to fight, and that made things a little less certain.

Villeprieux returned to the camp, dismounted from his horse and went straight to his tent, calling out orders for all groups leaders to meet him there in ten minutes. *He doesn't look a very happy man*, Rosso thought as he glanced up. *And that's not good news for anyone.*

The men began to steel themselves to the realization that perhaps they were going to have to fight as news of their captain's return spread around the camp. Fighting was their profession, and the bounty promised to be a good one. If they had to fight, then it would be to the death. The mood in the camp changed from good humor to grim determination in a matter of minutes.

In Villeprieux's tent, his leaders listened to what he had to say. It was a simple message.

"There's good news and there's bad news," he began in his normal, casual manner. "The good news is that the Spanish informed me this morning that they won't leave the field of battle until every one of us is dead, dying or fled."

As he spoke, he studied each of his men. None of them flinched as all held his gaze.

"The bad news is that, during the night, they received more re-enforcements, which means that we'll be out-numbered, three to one."

This time, there was the sound of shuffling feet and the adjustment of a sword belt, but no one looked away from their captain's young face.

"One thing will save us today, and that's discipline. Stay close to each other and protect each other's backs. Any questions?" he asked.

Although several unspoken thoughts hung heavy in the air, none was uttered.

"Then, glory or death!" he cried unsheathing his sword and pointing it slowly to each one of them.

"Glory or death!" rang out from their mouths as they all unsheathed their swords.

And as the singing of their blades ceased, each of them returned to their troop to prepare for battle.

The site for the battle was chosen some weeks earlier. It was on a slight rise, overlooking a flat stretch, limited by a busy river on one side and a wooded area on the other. The

Florentine Commanders hoped the location would give them a slight advantage. When they lined up, they looked down to see the enemy form up, fronting the woods, the sun glittering on their weapons and armor. There seemed to be so many of them—too many to count. Tn the order went out and was passed down along the lineshe men shouted out the battle strategy.

"Just kill the one in front of you—that's all that matters."

The usual battle process began with self-affirming battle cries arising from both sides, alternating "I'm for Florence" and "I'm for Spain." The local mendicant Friar offered God's blessing for a speedy victory for the Florentines at the same time that his Spanish confrere did the same for the Spanish camp.

However, once the rush to destruction and maiming began, the shouts gave way to screams and the sound of metal smashing on metal. Inevitably, the screams reigned supreme, interlaced with the calls, begging for help, and then the pervading sound of silence, horror, along with the terrible stench of death.

Death on the battlefield had a distinct odour—warm with a sweet essence, accompanying by the pall of fear, pain, and deep fatigue that reached into the soul. Those left standing could be best described as survivors rather than victors. Even while some gave occasional shouts of triumph, they were more happy to be alive than all else.

Rosso was not meant to be a player in such events, but when the disaster began to take shape, he realized he had no choice. Taking up two weapons from the few that were left behind, he looked for Villeprieux's banner above the tumult, becoming worried when he saw it on the periphery of the battle. Thinking that his friend had been captured, he gave no heed to self-preservation and headed deep into the tumult to aid his dearest friend.

He grew up accustomed to the sight of spilled guts and spurts of blood. For him, it came as no surprise to see how much blood could come from any beast. On that day, however, it was the faces of the bested men that haunted him. He witnessed their looks of disbelief as the power of great warriors transformed to childish terror as they fell back, mesmerized by the gush of blood coming from a slashed leg or a severed arm. Then, whilst sitting like rag dolls in the bloodied mud, they spouted final fountain of blood from their necks as their heads were cut clean from their bodies.

Rosso decided that avoiding direct confrontation was the best way to approach Villeprieux's ragged group. As he came closer, he heard his captain's once gently mocking voice, screaming.

"Retreat, Retreat. All is lost. Retreat!"

His ever-dwindling band, already showing the first signs of fear, became weaken at the knees when they heard his desperate cries. But standing tall in the middle of that awful destruction, the gentle Dom remained by Villeprieux's side.

The sight of the Dom was seared into his mind as the sky went suddenly white. In that instant, Rosso became aware that something terrible had happened to his back. As he twisted to see the cause of the searing pain, he saw a massive club descend in a slow arc of motion directly toward his head.

The color of the club that smashed into his skull reminded him of an olive tree he had played under when he was very young, and in that long, suspended moment—as he tried to recall who else he was playing with—life stopped, and his mind knew no more.

The place his mind occupied was not black. There were no dreams to color the moment, if indeed it was a moment, because time had ceased to exist. The very act of being ceased to exist, with nothing to mark time, its length, breadth, height or width. That nothingness could have been a second or a million years. For Rosso, it was all the same.

When he finally woke up, all was changed and silent. For a moment, he thought he might be dead, but then a staggering pain in his shoulder and another running down the length of his back reminded him of his earthly existence. A covered face appeared in the corner of his vision, coming close and whispering in his ear.

"It's okay. You can go back to sleep now. You're safe here."

With that, the pain screaming in his head caused him to black out again, but this time, he dreamed. In his dream, he saw Villeprieux in the distance, riding towards the Spanish army with his sword raised, laughing as he went. Rosso was trying to reach him, but all his movements were slowed by the deep mud he was trudging through. His voice seemed to be strangled in his throat.

Next came a woman who appeared to be ripping his arm off whilst all the time murmuring.

"It's okay now. You're safe with me."

When finally a deep dreamless sleep arrived, he blessed its dark, embracing arms.

He had been lying awake for a few minutes, watching the motes dance in sunlight that lanced in through a gap in the shutters. Some danced their jig in a disordered fashion, slowly sinking into the dark, whilst others ascended rapidly, like a soaring spark from a wood fire.

He wondered what made that one mote different, and what marked that one minuscule mote out for its unique and glorious moment. He watched bemused as it reached its zenith at the very limit of the light, and then disappeared.

"Well, it's good to see you awake at last. For a moment I thought you were going to sleep your life away," a soft female voice said from out of the gloom.

He adjusted his eyes to focus in the direction of the sound and saw her sitting in the corner, watching and waiting for him to wake.

"Don't move too much, because you've got a lot of healing to do yet. You've got a badly broken shoulder, and a deep wound in your back. Thankfully, it doesn't look like anything serious has been cut or punctured, but it must be kept clean, or else."

As she spoke, her voice trailed off. He was unsure whether her words were a threat or a warning.

"Where am I?" he asked. "And who are you?"

Though his voice was thick and weak, his lips were parched for want of water.

"Too many questions, young man, and the answers won't make any difference right now, not until you get some strength back," she answered. "All I ask of you is to trust me, which is a big ask, and I appreciate that, but it's the best and only option you have. So whilst I get you some water, you just lie there and thank your lucky stars that it was me that found you."

Rosso needed no reminding of the murderous, pillaging camp followers that seemed to appear like foul parasites at every battle fought in that god-forsaken country. As the mysterious woman left, Rosso decided to trust her and allowed himself to drift back to sleep.

His pattern of drifting off repeated itself for what seemed to be a few days, but by the time he was able to walk unaided. Through asking questions, he discovered that he had been with the woman for three weeks. She told him that he'd been, slipping in and out of consciousness and fighting off an infection that could have ended his life. By that time he, was familiar with the little cabin where the woman lived. It was stone, with an old thatch that was still sound. There was a single stool by the front half-door, where he liked to sit and feel the midday sun on his skin.

One day, as he sat on his little throne to admire his new-found kingdom, he paused to observe the strange woman who rescued him. He wondered why no one else had appeared. It seemed odd to him that she always kept her face partially covered, as if hiding something. Then he saw the bell on the floor next to the wash-up bucket, which stood on the table by small kitchen window. Thinking he'd escaped one nightmare, only to land in another, he cried out in horror.

"You've got leprosy!"

"Well, you're a smart young man," she replied. "Now, what makes you think I might have something so terrifying as leprosy?"

When she took a step towards him, eyes glinting, she emphasized that horrifying word.

"The bell by the door—no one ever *comes* here, and you've always got your face covered. Keep away from me!" he cried, holding his thin arms out towards her.

"It's a bit late for all that, isn't it?" she said as she removed the bucket and hopped onto the vacated space left behind on the table.

She smiled, her eyes gleaming impishly.

"After all, I've been feeding you food. I've been washing your skin, and changing your dressings for some weeks now. If I've got leprosy, as sure as night follows day, you've got too it by now!"

Swinging her legs back and forth playfully, she held his eyes in her gaze. After a long, theatrical pause, she continued.

"But don't worry—I haven't got leprosy. Mind you, it does comes in very handy for others to *think* that I've got it, because it keeps prying eyes well away from me and my place—which by the way, is also a very lucky thing for you too, all things considered."

She pushed her hair up under her veil while watching Rosso in silence.

In his weakened state, Rosso was confused. He slid down against the wall onto the floor, shaking his head, his right hand still clutching the door latch. It seemed a fog had taken up residence in his brain, blurring all thoughts and images into one.

"Look," she said. "You were at death's door when I dragged you away from all the rest of the carrion in that terrible field, but I'm glad I did it. I'm glad you're still alive to tell your tale."

Her voice took on a softer tone.

"But I think the time's come to start being a little more open with each other. And as I appear to be doing all the talking, it's probably a good idea for me to start with my story."

With that, she gave Rosso a reassuring smile, relieving a tightly-wound spring of apprehension that was building in his mind. As the tension in his face relaxed, he smiled.

"Okay, you go first," he said. "And anyway, my story's pretty short: I went to help a friend, I got hit on the head. Good night world—end of story!"

The woman watched him release the latch as he pulled his knees up towards his chest. To him, it seemed the first time he had felt really safe—in all his living memory.

As he spoke, the shawl that covered her head and most of her face slipped away, down onto her shoulders revealing two remarkable features. She had the most beautiful, shoulder-length red-brown hair with soft curls that framed her pretty features perfectly. The second notable characteristic involved the lower half of her face, which was cratered by several pock-marked scars.

She studied his face as he looked upon her.

"Now you can see why people think I have leprosy. Most people can't tell the difference between the effects of small pox or leprosy. Not that it matters much, because fear has a terrible way of dulling the mind and spreading ignorance."

Rosso was fascinated, but he no longer feared her.

"I think you're beautiful."

Even as he said these words, he really didn't understand why he had said them. They just happened to come out of his mouth, and they just happened to be the truth. Both blushed, and then they both started laughing.

"You're a strange one! There's no denying that," she jibed. "With compliments like that, I owe you the obligation of telling you my name. It's Agnes—named after a saint who promised God never to stain her purity, and look what happened to me!"

As she spoke, unconsciously she put her fingers to her disfigured chin.

"But you have beautiful eyes, and beautiful hair too," Rosso declared, blushing again in the color of his own red hair.

"Rosso's my name, and it's pretty obvious why I was called that," he said trying to cover up his embarrassment.

Agnes smiled, continuing her story.

"I won't go over the early part of my life. Sometimes, I think I didn't really have a childhood…"

Her words seemed disperse into the air like the last note of a harp.

"Suffice to say, I live here alone, and I am largely left alone to my own devices because of my terrible leprosy. A friend told me many years ago that we grow into the name we were given at birth, and it's true! I believe in what the Agnes of old was trying to do, and for me, it's to live a simple, yet good life. Suffice to say, I live here alone, and I'm largely left alone to my own devices because of my terrible leprosy. When the opportunity arises, I try to help others as best I can."

She paused, as if trying to weigh whether the words were the right words, or whether they required further explanations. Nodding to herself, she took up her story again.

"There had been rumors for weeks that two armies were going to run into each other someplace hereabouts, and people began to become frightened. Armies mean thousands of hungry men and some of them are not only hungry for food—which puts the fear of God into most women in these parts of the world."

She paused, and with a deeply-wounded expression haunting her eyes, she continued.

"Even women who look like me aren't safe when those men are abroad."

Rosso felt his blood rage at the shadow that seemed to fill the room in those few-worded moments.

"I stocked up on provisions and didn't light any fires that might draw attention to my little cabin of peace and light, and I waited. It didn't take long. It was the birds that gave the first alarm, then the noise traveling over the hills seemed to irritate even the trees themselves, as if they recognized their own fate in the coming battle. Then it all went quiet."

She paused, as if re-living the memory.

"When I heard the shouts and then the roars, I knew it had started. I sat here crying, because of the stupidity and madness of it all—as if any one of those lives that were lost or scarred would make the slightest of difference to kings or dukes a thousand miles away? What a terrible waste it was!"

Tears formed like glistening orbs in the corner of her eyes, sliding down her cheeks, occasionally pausing to bless one of the reminders of her own past battles.

"When the noise died down and the shadows length- ened, I covered myself and crept out of the house staying close to the shadows. By the time I reached the killing field, it was already turning to dusk. I saw those awful human carrion-birds, feeding on their plunder, ripping rings off the fingers of headless corpses, knocking gold teeth out of mouths that would never shout again, and removing boots from near dead soldiers, who would never walk or march in these wooded hills again.

"There was a shadow, hovering near you, but it held no sword and it did not seem like the others. It—no he— knelt down next to you, lifting your head. Then he did the strangest of things; he gently returned it to its place on the ground. As he remained on one knee, I even imagined that I heard him say something, but then I think he must have heard me close by, because he suddenly stood and moved off deeper into the shadows… and he vanished like some sort of ghost."

It was obvious to Rosso that Agnes had been disturbed yet fascinated by this shadowy figure, and for that reason, he stored her account of it in his memory.

"I went over to see what he'd been doing and then I found you. I thought you were dead, because you had been left for dead, but when you stirred and moaned, I knew I had to get you away from the stench and all that needless destruction. I dragged you down to the river's edge and left you in some tall rushes, walking upstream until I found a decent sized log, which I floated down to you. Getting you over the log and keeping it stable at the same time was the hardest part of all, but once you were on, I pulled you as far upstream as I could, closer to my little cabin. I came home for the donkey and sled, and we went back to get the shattered wreck that you were, and brought you home. The rest you now know."

Agnes sat on the table and began to swing her legs again.

"So, that's the story of how you came to be here. Why you were there and why was I there—therein lies the mystery of our lives."

After speaking, she fell silent as they both retreated into the phantoms of their parallel thoughts. When all that could be heard was the cawing and scratching of rooks on the rooftop, Rosso told his version of the battle, and how the loss of his friends and companions was a bitter blow, but that Agnes's kindness and care for him had helped dull the deep pain of their loss.

The conversation moved to normal events, but the wounds caused by death take a long time to heal, and Agnes knew not to reopen those scars that were still so fresh and so tender.

Rosso was still a young man, and although he had experienced more of life than most do in three times his span of years, he was still young, and he was hungry.

"Filling your stomach has become a full-time occupation," Agnes said with a knowing smile.

"I'm a growing lad," he retorted. "And I've got a lot of catching up to do."

"Talking of catching," Agnes interrupted. "Isn't it about time you earned your keep and got out there and caught some food for us? Remember that I'm a mere weak woman, unused to such labors," she said in a voice heavily-laced with sarcasm.

"Point taken," said the one-armed hunter. "I'll set some traps and see what turns up. I don't suppose you have anything that I can munch on whilst I'm out there in the big wide world, fighting dangerous animals such as rabbits."

She gave him a chunk of bread, roughly torn from a stale loaf, and a couple of apples from her stock.

"That should keep you going until you're back. But take care—there are still fugitives from the battle, hungry and desperate, who wouldn't think twice about trapping and skinning a weedy cove like you," she warned, grinning.

Rosso took her advice seriously, because he knew what such people could do when cornered, and in his weakened condition, he didn't want to find himself trapped and totally defenseless, like an animal.

8

OF CLOISTERS
AND THE CLOTH

ROSSO STAYED with Agnes for what seemed to be many weeks, but neither knew for sure. Her increasing kindness to him fashioned a place in his heart that she would occupy for the rest of his life.

The room where he had awoken was one of two rooms in that little cabin, the other being the place where the fire warmed and fed them and where the stores were kept. Agnes's little bedroom, surrendered to the wounded stranger, had a small window that let in the bright rays of each new day. Its walls of stone spoke a silent strength, and the wooden door had wooden latch that opened and shut with a welcoming breath of air.

When Rosso was finally able to rise unaided, he'd insisted on making a litter for himself by the fire, restoring to his nurse the privacy of her own room. All the while, they came to an easy understanding of each other. Childhood memories came to Rosso, which he shared with Agnes, and in the telling of the stories, his wounded memories slowly healed.

His own battle wounds had transformed from the raw, threatening anger of physical pain to the white specters of shared, past horrors now marking his flesh, leaving his mental scars to mature into something else. The changes there were more subtle. TThey were no longer painful burdens they were when fresh, but nowas they had become his companions and mentors.

He spoke of little Anna and of Brother Damien, with his funny chin but beautiful heart. He spoke generously of Gino, who had re-found love with Maria when he least expected it. But when he came to the Dom, words failed him as a cold fist clenched his heart. Agnes watched all this, waiting patiently for the fist to relax so that the words would flow again. They came haltingly at first, watered with tears that were matched by hers. But for a brief moment, the Dom lived once again in that safe warm haven.

He spoke too, of Villeprieux, with his wild enthusiasm for life and his total inability to take anything seriously for any great length of time. His good looks and natural flair for leadership made him into the wonderful friend that he was—at least in Rosso's eyes. When he recounted all the great things about him to Agnes, she smiled and took it all in, but there was a slight reservation that made Rosso halt.

"Can't you see what a fine man he was and what a huge loss he is?"

Agnes commented, her voice soft.

"It's strange that a man with so many talents and gifts should seemingly waste his life as a mercenary. Couldn't someone with such a good, quick mind have perhaps done a little bit more with his life?"

She tried to be tactful, but Rosso was insistent.

"Come on, Agnes, he's a hero!" he asserted, attempting to raise Villeprieux's character in her wise estimation. "He stopped more fights than we actually got into by parlaying with the enemy for peace before any battles were fought, and he probably saved hundreds of lives as a result."

The earnestness in his voice moved her to nod in agreement, although she quietly thought, *I wonder what were the terms of those peace deals?* But she kept her own counsel out of her respect for the guileless young man.

His wounds were healed and his strength returned. Their lives developed a familiar routine, although they were still very wary of chance of strangers who might stumbling onto their abode. Rosso baited his traps and set his lines in the stream each day, whilst Agnes kept the house clean and baked bread when there was flour to be found.

She had contacts with the local farmers, who exchanged eggs, flour or milk for mending work she did, or for her returning lost sheep or cattle that had taken an urge to explore the wider world. Agnes and the farmers knew that it was not a healthy option for beast nor man to wander, when wolves and wild dogs roamed. Yet those threats were nothing compared to those human scavengers for whom life held no value at all.

Agnes was able to read, which was a surprise to Rosso.

"When I was growing up, the only person I knew who could read was Brother Damien. Villeprieux could read too, so you're in exalted company," he said with a grin.

"All I have is the Bible and a few pamphlets," she replied. "But what I have is at your service."

She began to teach him to read. In return, he taught her the language of Villeprieux, with whom he had spent so much time, and to whom there was only one real language— French.

"*Il n'y a pas un autre langue dans tout le monde!*" he said with flamboyance, whilst giving a deep bow.

"And believe me, he could teach as well as he could wield a sword," said Rosso

"Perhaps he might have made a better ambassador than a mercenary," she murmured.

So between reading and writing on his part and learning French on her part, their days were full. Laughter was often their third companion. One day, when they were sitting on the ground with their backs to the cabin wall, taking in the warm autumn sunshine, Agnes asked what Rosso intended to do with his life.

"You've got a quick mind, you can read and write and you speak fluent French. What do you see yourself doing now?"

She let the answer hang in the air whilst she continued sewing.

"I could very well ask you the same question," he responded, giving her a dig in the ribs.

"Stop that," she said, as she gave back as good as she got.

Settling back into the silence, Rosso thought a moment and answered.

"I hear there's a new university in Pisa, which the Medici family founded. I thought I might give that a try, or perhaps I could go to Rome to study at one of the monasteries there—not that I have a calling or anything like that. I've always thought that I'd like to marry and have a family of my own one day. I think I'd make a good father."

He stopped talking and stared into the distance. After a moment, he continued.

"When I was very small and I did something wrong, and even when I hadn't done something wrong—there was a room next to the boning room of the butcher's shop, where my father used to store all the bones from the carcasses. He'd store them there until the smell got so bad that he had to do something with them, and the only thing he could do with those fly-blown, rotting bones was to drop them into some disused swamp a long, long way from the village, because the stink was so awful. Anyway, when he caught me and wanted to punish me, he'd lock me in that room with all those bones."

The gentle evening breeze rustled the long grass near the cabin, but Agnes remained silent.

"I was so scared, and I used to beat at that door until my little fists bled, and I cried and cried until the only refuge I ever got was when I fell asleep. When I woke up, it was always better, because it was dark and the smell wasn't so bad. But then I could hear things sniffing and scratching around outside the door, creatures smelling out the carrion that was all around me.

"And when my brother let me out, he used to tease me about how I was a cry baby and how that I should sleep with the dogs because I wet my bed at night. These aren't the memories any child should have, and that's why, should the good Lord allow it, I'd move Heaven and Earth to make sure that my child had only happy memories of growing up in any house I lived in."

Agnes saw the tears in his eyes as he finished his sorry tale. She sat there, like a loving sister, and waited for his thoughts to return to the present. She began with a new subject.

"Pisa sounds exciting, but it's still a Medici stronghold, and they may not like the idea of a renegade Venetian mercenary turning up and asking to join their new university. Rome might be a better option for you, because it's so much bigger, and because no one will know you there. It could be a whole new start for you."

She unpicked a stitch that had somehow become a knot.

"I had a friend, many years ago—a very dear man—who went to Rome. He's a monk in one of the monasteries there, but really he's more a teacher than a priest. We still write to each other. Perhaps I could write to him and ask him for his advice?"

Rosso turned toward her.

"Do you remember me telling you about little Anna?"

"Of course I do. You think I'd forget someone so very precious to you?" she said with no reproach in her voice.

"She was such a gorgeous little creature, and I loved her very much—and she loved me too."

He paused, his eyes falling on Agnes.

"And I'm beginning to think that, if she'd lived, she'd be just like you—kind, caring, and always wanting to bring the best out of people."

He reached over, placing his hands on her shoulders.

"Thank you for your help, new sister of mine. You've saved my life, healed my wounds, and now you've given me new hope. It's settled then. Let that be the course I take. You'll write to Rome and see what your friend shall have to say. Then, if they accept me, I'll go there to study and make you the proudest sister the world has ever known."

On hearing his words, Agnes beamed back at him with soft eyes, and yet her heart refused to follow her head as he continued.

"Let's embrace on that, dearest of all sisters, and wherever I might go, I'll always write to you, and tell you of my progress and adventures. And you must write to me and tell me all about you, too."

They embraced and pledged their friendship to each other, as brother and sister, with Rosso's dreams and visions of a grand and glorious future overshadowing the very treasure he already had.

Agnes wrote her letter, and after it was dispatched to Rome, there was a small shift in the balance that was their daily life. Rosso moved about with increased energy as he studied hard at reading and writing, describing what he might do when he arrived in the great city of Rome.

Agnes, for her part, was as warm and understanding as ever, rejoicing in his new-found direction in life. But whilst the one who enters on a great adventure will often gain the most attention, it is the one who stays behind who is the greater hero. Living an anonymous life while watching the one you love depart takes endless courage.

The days stretched into weeks until one day a reply came from Rome. Her friend indicated he would be glad to help. In his letter, he apologized for his tardy reply and related how he had suffered from a minor health issue that took longer than expected to recover from.

"Be careful in Rome, Rosso," said Agnes upon reading the letter. "There are so many contagions in that place. I do hope you will take good care of yourself."

He held her by the shoulders, speaking into her shining eyes.

"But dear sister of mine, you have me so healthy now that there are no foul humors in all of Rome that would dare approach this restored body that my Agnes has so lovingly blessed!"

Then the day of parting came. He had a strong staff for the journey, food to help him through the first few days and coins in his pocket to help get him as far as Rome. Despite his great enthusiasm for the adventure, Rosso was not insensitive to leaving Agnes behind in her old isolation.

"Are you sure you won't come with me to Rome?" he asked again, and again she refused.

"This is my place, and this is where I should be."

She couldn't put into words why it had to be, and yet both knew it was her vocation to live out her gentle life in a place of peace and solitude.

"I'll write as soon as I get to Rome," he assured her. "And if ever you need me, you only have to send a message, and your loving brother will come to you straight away."

Even as he spoke, he knew that she never would do such a thing. Saying it made him feel better.

"I'll miss having to look after you," was the closest she came to telling him the truth.

"And I'll miss being able to protect you, too," said Rosso feeling a strange emotion tugging at his heart.

They embraced before Rosso shouldered his load and left. He looked back four times on his way to the bend in the road, and each time, Agnes seemed to get smaller, but by the time he disappeared around the bend, she had occupied a large space in his empty heart.

As for Agnes, she watched him vanish from sight, but she sent secret armies in his wake to protect and guide him on his new mission in his young life.

✦ ✦ ✦

The route south to Rome took Rosso through the hills and countryside where the mists often hung over the fields, leaving them damp and glistening with dew. Cobwebs became jewels to sparkle in the hedgerows, and low flying larks sang to him along the way. The road was damp and deep-rutted by carts, which made the going slow. His boots were soon coated with a cloying clay, which he stopped to scrape off when his legs tired from the extra weight.

9

ROME

HE HAD MANY days to think about Agnes and of all her kindness to him. He thought of how she'd saved his life; a life that had held no relevance to her, and yet she had risked her own to drag him away from the battle and nurse him back to life. But her kindness, goodness and wise council had enriched his life. He smiled to himself as he relived all the memories. With those thoughts in his head and the knowledge that Agnes would always be there for him, he approached the escarpment that overlooked the plains that led to Rome.

The Eternal City was barely visible in the haze, but the stench of Rome pervaded the winds that blew from the coast. Rosso lingered on the escarpment for a few days, an invisible hand restraining him from descending onto those plains and the unforeseeable challenges that awaited him. It was cooler up on the high slopes.

He took the time to wander the ruins of Hadrian's villa and the newly built Villa D'Este, with its famous fountains. He had never seen the likes of those ancient structures and marveled at how they had stood the test of time, whilst those who had created them had been dust and ashes for centuries.

Vanity and greed had been the driving forces behind those grand villas, which peered proudly across the plain towards the melting pot that was Rome. The power of a Caesar on one side, or the infamous ego of a Duchess on the other caused them to be erected by sweat and blood, spilt into their walls and their foundations. At present, Caesar's palace was a crumbling mausoleum, looted over time, whilst the extravaganza that was the Countess's playground had become the summer retreat for a rich Cardinal and his mistress.

Eventually, Rosso tired of such overt opulence and ventured down the plain to seek a new life in the strange and ancient city on the edge of the sea.

The wheels of passing carts, trundling through well rutted tracks, made flinty sounds. The livestock trudged along with their several sounds: the bleat of the lambs on a wain, the baas of sheep in a flock, the occasional bullock-bell, metallically warning of the close proximity of a yoked pair of oxen, and the bray of stubborn mules, refusing to obey irate owners. These farmyard cacophonies increased in intensity as Rosso approached the gates of Rome.

The tide of humanity flowed in and ebbed out. Each one had arrived with a dream, and yet many were forced to leave, awaking from nightmares. Rosso joined that stream of living humanity and mixed his smell with the intoxicating brew of scents that enveloped him. Agnes had given him the address of a monastery on the hill that overlooked the Colosseum. Going through the Porta Di Roma, under the gaze of the guards, he headed down the cobbled lane-ways towards his goal.

The throng of people grew thicker as he went. He heard speech in accents that seemed to sound familiar, though they were incomprehensible. There were others there whose words were as strange to him as the many hues of their skin. Some wore clothes that matched their exotic speech. A monk of the Benedictine order struck up a conversation with him as he walked.

"You look like you're new to Rome, brother," he said in a friendly tone that reflected his contented features.

The monk was prone to interweave his periods of speech with periods of humming, and yet both his voice and his hum were very pleasing to the lucky listener's ear.

"Just arrived," said Ross having been warned by Agnes to not give too much information away to strangers—whatever cut of cloth they were. The monk hummed a pretty tune Rosso liked. Compared to the singing he'd heard in taverns, the monk had the voice of an angel.

"Rome is an entrancing, Mistress, my friend," the monk continued. "She can beguile the best of souls and leave them destitute in the gutter. She can fascinate, with all her glory, yet leave you hungry for something of real substance. And yet …"

He drifted, humming a mournful tune that would swirl inside Rosso's head long after they had parted.

"May I be so bold as to ask where you are heading?" he asked.

"Santa Maria Maggiore."

"Well, it'll be difficult to miss that," the monk said in a happy, antiphonal hum of praise. "It's the biggest church on any of the hills around Rome, and not even an earthquake could shake those magnificent foundations," he laughed. "In fact, you'll often find me there, with some of my brothers. It really is a magnificent place, and I'd be honored to show you around if you'd humbly allow me the pleasure? Are you in Rome for long?"

"I'm honestly not too sure," replied Rosso, relaxing into the conversation with his affable new friend. "It's been a long journey and an even longer story behind it, but I've come here to learn, and my dear sister friend has given me the name of someone who might be able to guide me."

"And may I enquire of the name of this person," sang the monkish man he walked. "After all, I can modestly claim to know quite a few souls who reside in that glorious edifice."

Smiling, he hummed hosanna.

"His name is Father Alphonsus," Rosso said after the noise of the city palled enough for them to hear each other.

"Ahh, blessed Alphonsus!" the monk said, resorting to a mournful hum, "He's had a big cross to bear since that last illness of his. The poor fellow. Did you know him before?

"Before what?" Rosso asked. "What happened to him?"

"Oh, forgive me," his companion replied. "I thought you might have known him before he had the stroke."

Seeing Rosso's confusion he continued.

"He was always so well, and that this should happen to him came as quite a shock to everyone, especially the dear fellow himself. He's a magnificent teacher and had the voice of an angel, but that's all gone now. He can still get around with a stick, but it's a real struggle for him. And he can still understand everything that you say to him. It's just that he can't speak any sense at all. It comes out as complete gibberish."

Having passed on this distressing information, he hummed his way into a quiet, reflective moment whilst remembering his old friend, Fr Alphonsus.

"The amazing thing is that he has taught himself to write with his other hand, although it's not as good as before. The strain of it is one thing, but you can see what a real trial it is to him to slow down the learning of others. But then you see, teaching is not about passing on facts and information. With knowledge comes suffering, and Fr Alphonsus is the epitome of both."

Just then, the ragged remains of the Colosseum came into view. It was nothing like Rosso imagined. In his mind, the Colosseum was a magnificent amphitheater where the Christians fought the gladiators or were eaten by lions in front of vast, baying crowds. The edifice that rose before his eyes, whilst still a massive construction, had the appearance of being used as a giant quarry, which in fact it really was.

"Cats."

"Pardon?" Rosso asked.

"Cats live there mainly. We Romans like our cats, and they appear to like our Colosseum, which is a good thing, because they do keep the population of rats under control. With so much rubbish in the streets, you see..." and he hummed off to a celestial spot in which Noah led all the cats and rats into his ark!

"Cats make me sneeze," said Rosso. "And by the way, my friends call me Rosso. My parents did too, but that's another story."

"I'm Julian—like the calendar," he said with a dancing light in his eyes. "Santa Maria is just over there," he pointed, "and we'll be there in ten minutes. I'll get someone to take you to Fr Alphonsus when we arrive. I've got one or two things to do this morning."

"You've been very kind to me. Are all Romans as nice as you?" Rosso asked.

"Let's just say that, in this case, the exception makes the rule," he replied. "Be on your guard, young Rosso, because a red-headed country lad could easily find himself in trouble in this eternally greedy city."

He hummed a mournful psalm until they arrived at Santa Maria Maggiore, that great monument to God, funded in the main by many of His earthly yet penitent bankers.

✝ ✝ ✝

Rosso had never seen anything as magnificent in all of his short life. The soaring, vaulted ceilings, with their mosaics of the Mother of God; the high arched windows, with all their stained glass glory; the altar, surrounded by marbled wonders and artworks, created by the most talented painters in all of the Papal States. They all seemed to him to come together in a seamless exultation that cried out the genius of mankind and the wonder that is their God.

"This way, young man," said a voice behind him. "Brother Julian has asked me to lead you to Fr Alphonsus."

Dragging himself away from the visual splendors before him, Rosso followed his guide out of the church and into the building next door. But though it looked plain and humble on the outside, inside were more works of great wonder, more carvings of the Virgin, more statues of the saints and crucifixes, depicting Christ in many differing states of his final agony!

But then they found themselves back in the sunlight again, crossing a small courtyard, with its central fountain sprinkling its sound of beneficent peace to anyone who would stop and listen. On the far side was what appeared to be a long stable, with several plain wooden doors.

His guide knocked on one of those and entered. Rosso followed. The room reminded him of Brother Damien's cell, with its white walls and rush floor mat. An old man with a shock of white hair sat a desk by the small window that overlooked the garden. He wore a black robe, and a wooden stick with a well-worn top sat against the wall next to him. He finished what he was scratching on the vellum before him, put down his pen and turned to greet his visitors.

Rosso was struck by the intensity of his eyes, with brown penetrating orbs.

I felt like a small boy who'd been caught stealing an apple, he later wrote to Agnes. *But then he smiled his lopsided smile, and my greatest wish was to rush into his arms and lose myself in those black robes knowing that finally, I would be safe.*

Fr Alphonsus offered Rosso his left hand, the other being held lifeless in a sling. He indicated with his eyes for Rosso to take the stool next to him and passed him the vellum.

"Welcome dear friend of my dear friend Agnes. To have known her is to have sat in the shade of peace and breathed in its goodness. We'll begin our studies tomorrow. Today, I ask you just to experience Santa Maria Maggiore. Do not ask questions. Do not even think—just experience. Until tomorrow."

Holding out his hand for the vellum, he gently inclined his head, and Rosso reflected his movements as he left that saintly cell.

Rosso returned to the church, walking around it, trying to absorb the beauty that threatened to overwhelmed his senses. He touched the mighty soaring pillars that so many other hands had touched before him. His feet touched marble flagstones, marking the remains of those who'd achieved great fame or dared great deeds in life. He watched the candles flicker their light and create wondrous shadows on darkened walls, before sputtering and dying, adding a new layer to the depths of the embracing darkness.

Whilst he was deeply absorbed into the enormity of it all, he heard something that made the hairs on his skin arise with pure joy at its heavenly perfection. The tenor voice came through the air like a shimmering cloak and enveloped him with wonder, whispering secrets of life beyond words. The very walls of the cathedral embraced the joyous tones, and every eye on every painting seemed to Rosso, for that moment, to be gazing toward the choir stalls. Even the candles bowed in stunned admiration and nodded, as if acknowledging that the moment was special for them as well.

Then it stopped, and though Rosso tried to hold onto the physical sensation, he felt the color in his life had ebbed away. He looked toward the dimly-lit stalls and made out the figure of Julian, taping a sheaf of music into shape and slipping it under his arm.

Rising and forgetting to even pause to bend his knee before God, he rushed up the nave to greet his friend.

"Was that really you? It was so beautiful that I thought I must have died and gone to heaven."

The words tumbled from his mouth. He paused, holding Brother Julian by the shoulders, a gleaming tear in his eye.

"Thank you, Julian. That was the most beautiful thing I've ever heard in all of my life. Thank you."

His merry friend let his eyes do the laughing. He bowed.

"It's my gift from the Almighty, and all I have to do is use it. But I thank you for your kindness." Then like a small boy he added, "Have you eaten yet?"

Agnes had told him that life in Rome revolved around two things—talking and eating, although many in that glorious city were often one meal away from the nipping pangs of starvation. At the moment, Rosso's stomach informed him that he must be almost be a Roman too, as he hadn't eaten since he'd arrived.

So he followed along happily after Julian, who led him to the small cell where he lived. Rosso was expecting to find food there, but his jovial friend smiled.

"The food here is, how shall I put it?—akin to hair shirts and ashes."

Giving Rosso a wink, he reached under his mattress to retrieve a leather pouch and tucked the small sack into his cassock, headed back out the door, with Rosso in close pursuit.

"There's a little tavern within walking distance from here, which is just far enough away to be discreet, where they…" and he searched his memory for the right word whilst humming a sacred hymn, "Let's just say, they reward my skills with some tasty pasta and excellent wines."

"So you sing for your supper?" Rosso asked entering the fun of the conversation.

"The saints preserve me, no!" Julian protested. "The Bishop would hear of that far too quickly, and then my stomach would pay the price for my indiscretions! No, I teach the landlord's daughter music," he said, with a playful look in his eyes. "She's quite a gifted student, but it's too soon to tell how good, as she's still very young. But I believe she holds some promise, and her voice is sweet, too."

He trilled off down the cobbled alleyways until they came to a break in the houses, where he paused, looked in both directions, and he disappeared into the gloomy darkness of the lane way.

A battered board swung on rusty hinges above the low door, informing lost souls who may have stumbled into its presence that it was "La Villa Di Famiglia." Julian entered without pausing, but Rosso felt nervous about what he might find inside the seedy looking establishment. He hesitated for a moment, before stepping out of the dirt-littered alleyway and into a wall of country kitchen aromas.

The mixed scents of rosemary, garlic, thyme and virgin olive oil made him giddy with hunger. Then he was struck by another wall, in the form of a very large hand striking him on the back.

"You're very welcome, my young friend."

When he looked back, Rosso thought he might be dreaming, because the person who said them was Julian himself—but it *wasn't*, because Julian was standing next to him. Rosso felt like a mannequin at a fair, turning his head from side to side, with his mouth wide open, whilst the twins' rosy features beamed with delight at his confusion. They embraced him.

"I'm sorry, Rosso," said Julian, wiping tears of laughter from his eyes. "Gian is my younger brother—by three minutes, and this is his taverna."

The shouting from a young girl interrupted his words.

"Uncle Julian!" she screamed as she threw herself into his arms and smothered him in hugs and kisses. "You didn't tell us you were coming, but I hope you brought me a present!"

"Oh my dear," he said, feigning regret. "I left in such a hurry that I forgot …"

The girl's serious young face looked deep into his eyes as she held his chubby cheeks between her two small hands.

"Uncle, you know monks shouldn't tell lies."

As she tapped his cassock, she felt a bulge in his pocket.

"Come on, Uncle," she demanded. "What are you hiding here?"

"Oh that," he said casting his eyes towards heaven. "That's something for a poor young girl whose uncle never brings her any presents!"

He pulled out the pouch and handed it to his delighted niece. Undoing the strings, she reached in and pulled out a small hair comb.

"Oh, Uncle Julian, it's beautiful!"

Tossing back her hair she, placed the comb in her black tresses, flouncing her head from side to side, whilst those around admired her beauty. Gian stood watching with enormous pride, whispering to his brother.

"For a destitute friar, you always seem to find something special for that young lady."

Julian smiled.

"God hears the cries of the poor."

"Mama, come and see what Uncle Julian has brought for me," she shouted through an open door.

She was soon surrounded by not only her mother, who might have been taken for an older sister, but by several other young children who tumbled out of the door behind her. Watching from his place by the door, Rosso's beamed at the sight of the loving family who had transformed that small space into a world of laughter.

"Come on through, friend of Julian," Gian called.

"Let me take you to where all the action really happens."

Leading the young man through another doorway, they entered a small courtyard, where small round stools surrounded small round tables, and where small flowers smiled in earthenware pots.

"This is our humble restaurant," he indicated with the air of a man who might be surveying a Ducal Hall. "But as you can see, we're shut today. And the reason we're shut today is because it's a very special birthday today, isn't it, Julian?"

His twin was trilling like a lark as he answered.

"I believe it is, dear brother. And I believe that it's our birthday."

At that, all the children began to shout and sing happy birthday to the two very happy men. After calling for volunteers to help her in the kitchen, Gian's wife led most of the children off to help prepare the festive meal. Gian found the few remaining imps who chose to hide behind a statue and sent them, giggling, on to their mother, leaving the men to finally talk in peace.

"Let me introduce Rosso to you, dear brother," Julian announced.

He told what he knew of Rosso's tale before slapping his forehead and exclaiminghe paused.

"Why am *I* telling you all this, when the young lad has a perfectly good voice of his own?"

So Rosso told his own tale.

Both brothers were moved by what they heard, even shedding tears when they heard of his little sister's untimely death. Even the noise in the kitchen became stopped what they were doing to listen as that happy household seemed to be swallowed by a sorrowful maw.

"Food is ready!"

Those magic words that dispelled the shadows, and instantly the square blue sky above their heads seem clearer and brighter, whilst the smell of a delicious meal drove all shreds of anxiety away. The children tumbled back into the courtyard and bringing with them thethe food filled the small round tables before Julian offered words of gratitude to his all-seeing God.

Later in the day, in the quiet of his small cell, Rosso was able to reflect on those precious few hours around the happy tables. *Perhaps that's what real families are like*, he thought to himself, and then he chuckled at the banter between the twins:

"*He* can't sing," Julian said, nudging his brother.

"And *he* can't bake," returned Gian.

"But I can *eat*," Julian laughed, picking up a crusty loaf and breaking it over his plate.

"And I can propose a toast," Gian countered. "*To family!*"

They all clinked their glasses, shouting, "Family!" Rosso's voice was the loudest and sincerest of all!

10

HOLY ORDERS

CONSIDERING THAT Fr Alphonsus had suffered a serious stroke, he still had a mighty mind! It grieved all who knew him to watch him move so ponderously around the small, confining room, but his mind roamed large and his greatest joy was to infuse information into the minds of willing students. As Rosso had a huge thirst for knowledge, they soon learned each other's minds.

Because he was fluent in Parisian French, Rosso quickly found himself with a small paying job working for Italian merchants who required translation from French customers. So it wasn't long before Wword of his work found its way to the ears of the powerful who walked the labyrinthine corridors Vatican itself.

But it was the joy of studying under his frail friend, Alphonsus, that gave him the greatest joy. He began each day with a walk through the majestic Church of Santa

Maria and listened to the voices of the choir, which stirred something in his heart, causing both delight and confusion.

"There's so much beauty, yet so much ugliness in the world; so much happiness and so much suffering; so much gaudy opulence, and yet so much poverty. How could a loving god allow all of this?" he asked his teacher on a daily basis.

Alphonsus gave one of his lopsided smiles, shrugged his shoulders and pointed to the crucifix on the wall, as if that barbaric torture could provide some clue to the answers. As time passed, Russo thought that perhaps he might be called to a life in the Church.

He wrote long letters to Agnes, telling his "sister dear" of his inner turmoil. Yet when he went for walks through the marketplaces and saw all the pretty girls, another part of him whispered the joys of carnal pleasure and perhaps a life of married bliss with a brood of children.

✠ ✠ ✠

From his arrival in Rome he had been staying over the stables behind Santa Maria Maggiore, a place that distilled the many aromas of manure. He had grown accustomed to the noise of shouting and neighing and the rustling of the many rats that competed with the horses for the sacks of oats that made up Rosso's bed.

His teacher observed that sleep was a problem for his pupil, and after a few probing inquiries, he wrote down the answer: the Augustinian Friary was not far off, and they would take him in as a "guest," but it would also mean that Rosso would have to follow their rules.

The first rule concerned sharing common property, and it was an easy one for Rosso, who had no possessions to mention, but the other rules were more complicated. The rule of the Superior was absolute and demanded total obedience was far harder to swallow. For Rosso, such a rule brought back memories of a furious, fractious father, which triggered an immediate reflex to rebel and resist any such authority. Another rule dictated that idle talk and gossiping was not allowed, and "all feelings of pride and envy were suppressed, and brotherly love was enjoined." Rosso's understanding of sibling love was scant to say the least.

Next, nothing was to be sung, except that which was ordered, and fasting and abstinence were to be strictly observed.

"Who thought up that one?" he responded. "Most of us live that way anyway."

Finally, nothing offensive was permitted by their habit or gestures, and they were forbidden to look upon women. Such an edict for young men like Rosso was virtually impossible and made him question why God had created women in the first place—if men weren't even allowed to look at them.

Scouring the rules pinned to the door of his cell, he muttered to himself.

"I wonder what sort of twisted person wrote those rules?"

For his first act of independent thought, he wrote "*Amor vincit omnia*" underneath the last rule before leaving.

✛ ✛ ✛

Back on the streets of Rome, he felt alive. Although the setting was a testament to the struggle for human existence, he felt inspired that the people, regardless of their situations, carried such hope and happiness in their hearts. But heartbreak was everywhere, with abandoned children begging for a crust to survive on street corners.

Rosso felt for the little children, and as time went on, he never left the Friary without having something in his pockets for them. It was not long before he had a following amongst them and found that, whilst food that might keep them alive, what they really needed was love and acceptance. One day, a small ragamuffin called out to him.

"Pietro's found a pile a rags wot's aving a fit or summink," he snuffled, wiping his nose on his ragged sleeve.

"Who's Pietro, and what on Earth are you talking about?" Rosso asked.

"Pietro's a good bloke like you is, and e's found a bloke wot's in a real bad way. Come on, you gotta elp him—uvverwise, he might cark it."

He led Rosso by the hand into a dark doorway, where a tall thin man who held a long walking cane was indeed leaning over a shivering, ragged man. When the thin man looked up, Rosso glanced back into clear, kind, pale blue eyes.

"Thank you for coming," the thin man said, "although I'm not sure if we can do anything to help the poor man. He really is in a terrible state."

He glanced down at the man, dying on the ground.

"By the way, I'm Pietro. I've heard lots about *you* already. Don't worry, it's all good," he smiled.

His thin face seemed too small a canvas for such striking eyes.

"I'm Rosso, and I'm pleased to meet you as well, although it's a shame that we have to meet like this."

His eyes examined the sickly man, who groaned aloud.

"Do we know anything about him?"

He knelt down next to the poor wretch, attempting to ignore the dreadful stench he emitted.

"No," Pietro answered. "He just appeared overnight—no different to the thousands of others who appear overnight in doorways in this wonderful city of ours."

Pietro paused, leaning his pointed chin on the long cane.

"I could probably hazard a guess as to why he's here, but that wouldn't tell us who he is."

Rosso turned the man over to make him more comfortable. He was missing a hand and a bloodied rag covered the stump where the hand once was. The bandage around his head covered one suppurating eye socket, a sightless pit, weeping pus.

When Rosso rolled him to a sitting position, he froze with horror. The other eye looked lifelessly back at him— and in an instant, he knew that eye. It belonged to the Dom!

"Dom!" he shouted, tears filling his own eyes. "Dom, dear God! What have they done to your beautiful face and body? Dom—talk to me! Dom? Dom? Dom!"

He sobbed as he rocked his beloved friend back and forth in his arms.

"Dom, what have they done to you? Dom, my dearest Dom!"

Pietro and the boy looked on in silence, though Rosso felt the gentle pressure of Pietro's hand on his shoulder.

"I think perhaps we should take him somewhere where he can get cleaned up a little. Why don't you bring him back to my place? It's not far from here, and he can stay there for a few days until we can work out what to do next. I'll get a cart. He looks like he's a big lad, and it'll be much easier to wheel him than to try and carry him."

"He was much bigger when I last saw him," Rosso nodded wiping the tears from his eyes. "We spent years on the road together. He saved me after I ran away from home. He was such a good and kind person. Who could be so cruel as to do something like this?"

He lifted the arm with the missing hand. He looked up, exchanging an anguished look with Pietro before turning back to the ragged urchin. He cradled his friend whilst the boy went for a cart. When the boy returned, some kind passersby helped lift the Dom onto it, and they wheeled him to where Pietro lived, a few streets away.

Pietro only had one room, but it was clean and bright. He only had one bed, but it was fresh and comfortable. He only had one chair, but it looked as if Pietro had spent many a night sitting in it.

"What I have is at your disposal," Pietro said. "He can have my bed. I usually try to sleep in the chair. It's my back…"

✢ ✢ ✢

After they laid the Dom on the bed, they began to removing his rags. His body was badly scarred across the chest and the back. Some of the wounds were caused by swords and others by whips, but both had cut deep. Rosso and Pietro did the best that they could and left the Dom to rest. It was difficult to say whether he was asleep with his one eye open, or if he was in that place where only the severely wounded of spirit go, but he was somewhere beyond their reach.

"I'll go back to the Friary and talk with the apothecary to see if he's got any ointments we can use," Rosso announced.

"Take your time," Pietro nodded. "The poor creature isn't going anywhere. In fact, it's a miracle that he got himself here in the first place."

Taking his beads from his pocket, Pietro began to pass them through his fingers.

He noticed Rosso watching him.

"I got these from an old Arab. Clever people—those Arabs."

He settled into his chair to watch and wait as Rosso hurried back to the Friary.

"The Abbot's looking for you," the gnarled gatekeeper informed Rosso as he hurried through the studded wooden door. "And I don't think it's to wish you a good day either."

The gatekeeper spat on the ground, kicked some dirt over the spittle and locked the gate with a heavy iron key.

I wonder what he wants? Rosso thought as he made for the Abbot's room. He knocked and waited.

"Come!" a voice called from behind the door, and Rosso obeyed.

Inside, the Abbot was seated behind a wide desk, covered with parchments. Next to him was a lectern, on which there was a book of Holy Scripture, beautifully illuminated and positioned to catch the light from the casement window nearby.

The abbot, wearing a black surplice, had black hair, neatly tonsured with a shining dome. At that moment, his expression was black as well.

"Ah, Rosso," he began in a conciliatory tone. "Come in. I'm glad you could make time to meet with me," sarcasm edging into his voice. "You've been our guest for some time now, and perhaps it's time for you to make some important decisions about your future. I understand that you're gifted in languages and that you have a bright future academically."

He picked up some parchments, as if reorganizing them, and put them down. Rising from his high backed, ornately carved chair, he came around the desk, standing directly in front of the young man. He was tall, with ascetic features, and though he was freshly-scented with rose water, his breath smelt stale as he spoke.

There was something about the man's eyes that reminded Rosso of his father. The look of the man caused Rosso to stare, stony-faced back at him in just as the same way he'd done to his father.

"Either you advise me that you wish to be a postulant, or you leave," the Abbot said.

The only muscle that moved on his waxen features was the one that pinched his aquiline nose.

"And I wish to know by morning," he said peering at the dead eyes before him.

The spell was broken by the high pitched tingling of a silvered bell, which the Abbot held in his hand. Turning his back, the black-cowled master of all the black-cowled Friars retreated behind his grand desk, where he stood, drumming his fingertips along its gilded edge.

"Postulancy or penury," he smiled. "I pray God will guide you along the right path. You may leave now."

Rosso left in a cloud of confusion, passing the gatekeeper, whose gnarled smile announced that he had overheard their conversation through the keyhole. Rosso paced along the flagstones in the cool of the cloistered quadrangle whilst water trickled from the central fountain.

To stay on as a postulant meant that his education could continue. Perhaps that was what God was calling him to do anyway. But the unpleasant incense that came from the mouth of the Abbot reminded him that "Holy Church" was not all it appeared to be, and he was not overjoyed about being bound by the rigid ties of total obedience to the Abbot.

He needed to talk to someone. If only Agnes were there, she would have given him the wisest of advice, but it would take weeks before any letter could go and return from her. If he were to become a postulant, then she could no longer write to him.

Out of the depths of despair, a new thought came.

"Brother Julian! Now why didn't I think of that straight away?"

He had turned to go and find his friend to seek sane advice, when he remembered the Dom and telling Pietro he was going to the apothecary to get ointments for his wounds. How could he abandon his dear friend in his hour of need? There were too many decisions to make and so little time to think about them. *But it'll all become clear, once I've talked with Julian*, he thought.

He was walking toward the main gate when he heard a voice cry out.

"And where do you think *you* might be going?"

Looking up, he saw the gatekeeper approaching, with his bunch of iron keys jangling at his hip.

"I said, where do you think *you're* going?" he repeated. "'Cos the Abbot told me you ain't to go *nowhere*. He wants you to stay right here in the Friary till he sees yer tomorrow. So, it's the chapel for you, my young bucko, and there's no time like the present."

He stood between Rosso and the gate, daring the younger man to make a move toward it. Rosso tensed himself. For an instant, thought he would push the gnarled old root out of his way and go through that door forever, but something held him back. He exhaled, turned around and, brushing an imaginary fleck of dirt from his sleeve, he walked off toward the chapel.

The darkness of night can magnify the senses and the passions, while the cold light of dawn can strip them away. In the dark, thoughts became more ardent, fears became darker, and the sense of isolation more complete. Rosso had heard priests say that God lives in the darkness, because we are at our most vulnerable in the dark. *How much darker does it need to get before he shows himself* Rosso thought drawing his black cowl over his shivering, cold shoulders

At first, the gilded light from the guttering candles and the faces of holy people, gazing down at him from the frescoed walls, fueled his heart with sacred thoughts. But in the small hours of the night, along with fatigue and cold came the profound specters of doubt. Rosso had heard it said that God lives in the darkness, because that's when we are at our most vulnerable. *How much darker does it need to get before he shows himself* Rosso thought to himself, drawing the black cowl over his shivering, cold shoulders By dawn, he felt close to tears.

Then the choirs of birds began to sing, and the morning light gave color to the stained-glass windows, high above the altar. The light drove out the fear, and he made his decision.

In the hour after dawn he stood at the Abbot's door, feeling confident about his decision. The knock he made felt small and dulled by the ancient oak.

"Enter," the Abbot called.

He spoke without lifting his head from the parchment he was reading.

"Ah. You return. You've have made a decision?"

"I will stay if you will have me," Rosso announced.

"Then you'd better attend the Novice Master," the older man advised. "Close the door after you."

He scratched his signature on the parchment before him, sprinkled it with pepper, and blew the dust in the direction of Rosso, who turned and left.

"But don't expect me to obey all of your rules," Rosso said to himself as the latched clicked an end to their conversation. Clenching his jaw, he went to talk to the Novice Master.

Brother Bartholomew—*You can call me Bart if you want to, but not if the Abbot's within earshot*—was a kindly man whose flesh hung in folds over his face, like soft curtains. His nut brown eyes shone out over red, rheumy rims, from which the occasional tear coursed down a skin crease, giving him an air of great sadness.

But Brother Bart still had the enthusiasm of youth, and a disposition that belied his facial features. Over his many decades of watching boys and young men enter the Friary, he could tell the character of each postulant within hours of meeting with them. That made him happy, but it sometimes darkened his heart.

"*You* must be Rosso," he said. "Are you sure you want to become a postulant? You *do* understand what that means, I hope?" he asked, wiping an errant tear from his face.

Rosso paused for a moment whilst looking at this strange old apparition, thinking he saw a soul he could trust.

"I can give my heart to God, but my mind's a different beast, and I'm not sure whether it can be subdued into being a tame monk," he said, trusting the wise mentor to keep his confession. Brother Bart smiled, causing a small stream of tears to spill from his eyes.

"I believe that's the kind of honesty that God wants from us all," he said. "It's just that—not all monks would agree with you."

He gripped the young man's shoulders, giving him a reassuring shake.

"There are many here who say that obedience is everything, and *that's* what I say to most of my postulants. But then when you look at most of our great saints, they all started out as a pretty hopeless lot. However, the one thing they all had in common was that they all had great hearts, and in the end, God found *them*. I think that, between us, we can find a straight path in the midst of our crooked lives... *but according to the rules*."

He winked at Rosso.

"You'll need to have a haircut. Then you won't look as obvious in our little community, although with that red hair of yours—that might be easier said than done."

Patting Rosso on the back, he sat him down and shaved a tonsure into his head, so that when Rosso left the Friary later that day, even the gatekeeper had to look twice to reassure his gnarled brain that it was Rosso. The new novice glanced down, smiling to himself as he passed his nemesis and making straight for Pietro's lodging, where he found everything much the same.

"You've been busy," Pietro called out while still running his beads through his fingers. "But you didn't have to become a *monk* to get the information from the apothecary, did you?"

He smiled at his young friend.

"There's a story behind it all, but how's the Dom today?"

"Much the same as when we found him yesterday, but sweeter smelling, and he's had something to drink too. So considering all that he's been through, he's doing okay."

Rosso took the Dom's hand and squeeze it to reassure his friend.

"Has he said anything?" he asked.

"Nothing. He just lies there, looking at the ceiling with that empty look in his eye," Pietro answered.

There was silence in the room.

"I'd like to sit with him for a little while, if that's all right," Rosso said.

"Surely you can," Pietro replied while easing himself out of his chair. "My stomach is rumbling with unusual vigor, which means it must be fed, or I'll be the worse for ignoring it."

Taking his jacket from a peg behind the door he called back.

"Can I get you anything whilst I'm out?"

"Nothing. Thanks Pietro—you've done everything so far, so take your time."

Sitting next to the Dom's bed, Rosso lifted the poor man's hand into his own and held it next to his heart.

"We'll be fine. See you later."

Pietro examined the scene in his simple home, and turning, he closed the door behind him—as if it were a blessing upon the two inside. Some hours later, Pietro tapped his way down the street, leaning on his walking cane while trying to ignore the fierce, whip like pain shooting down his leg from his deformed and damaged spine. In his free hand, he ran the beads through his fingers at a furious pace, which was the only external sign he allowed himself of his internal torment.

Reaching the door of his lodging, he opened the latch and went in. Rosso had fallen asleep with his head on the Dom's chest, exhausted after his night long vigil and struggle. Then Pietro saw that the Dom's solitary eye was open and he was gazing at the freshly shaved tonsure on Rosso's head, which he was caressing so very lightly with his solitary hand.

At the rim of that gazing eye was a single tear, suspended like a jewel, and out of which shone a rainbow of lights. Instantly, that tear was matched by one on Pietro's cheek as he stood watching this beautiful scene. Then slowly, so very slowly, the Dom lifted his finger to his lips and his eye sought out Pietro's. The older man understood immediately and moved to his chair to wait for the young novitiate to wake from his deep sleep.

11

A HOLY SPIDER WEAVES
AN UNHOLY WEB

HEALING COMES in many forms. The physical
wounds can leave obvious physical scars, but the emotional
and mental ones are often so deep that they are unseen
and rarely fully heal. In the weeks and months that came,
the Dom regained his physical strength.

That he had just one hand was an annoyance more than
a hindrance. That he had one eye may have limited his
vision, but it deepened his compassion for those who had
no eyes. That he had been weak and wounded made him
more determined to be strong and independent. But the
Dom never mentioned a word of the battle or what had
happened to him or to their friend Villeprieux.

On the few occasions that Rosso spoke of that dreadful day of battle and death, the big man tensed and his eye
sparkled with horror. At the mention of Villeprieux's name,

he gave Rosso a bewildering look. It was as if the Dom was trying to say something so sad that the words had yet to be formed to describe what was inside his head.

But as the Dom groped his way back into the stream of life, an idea germinated in Rosso's mind. And when that idea became green-tinged with the Dom's increasing strength, he shared it with Brother Julian, and the two of them decided to form a small conspiracy.

Gian ran the family's small taverna, Gian's wife ran the kitchen, and their children ran their parents' lives in a way that only the children can. Raising a large family meant balancing the needs of their children with the needs of customers, so everyone helped where they could. On their meager income, they could not afford the wages for an extra *pair* of hands—but *one* hand—perhaps they could afford one. Thus a few weeks after the Dom had begun to roam the streets, helping those whom he could, Rosso and Pietro took him for a walk to meet Gian and his family.

There is always great satisfaction in finding a missing piece in a jigsaw that completes a particular pattern. The Dom fitted in with the family He was the gentle giant that the children needed for sharing, and he was the extra hand that Gian found so useful when it came to the heavier work around the taverna. The family cleared a small storage room to make space for him, and he settled in like a prince in a palace.

When Rosso was leaving one day on his way back to the Friary, the Dom stopped him and gave him a huge bear hug.

"Thank you. You're the best friend a man could ever have."

"I couldn't be more happy at seeing you so well even if the Abbot came down with a plague of boils" Rosso replied as he left the Taverna and head d off down the alleyway. He watched the young black monk with his red tonsured head disappear down the alleyway until he was gone.

It was during the latter part of the Dom's recovery that Rosso received an unexpected summons—to the Vatican to meet with a Cardinal Visconti for "discussions." Confused, he went to the Noviciate master.

"What do you think I should do? Who is this Cardinal Visconti? What does he want with me?" he asked while in his mentor's office.

"Visconti is from Milan," said his wise friend. "And being a Cardinal means things are never as they appear to be. Such are the machinations of our Holy Mother Church," he answered with in a wistful tone. "Just be very careful. The good Lord wisely gave us two eyes to watch with and two ears to listen with, but only one mouth. So watch and listen twice as much as you speak. But most of all, listen to the voice in the silence of your heart. To be fair to them, most are often good men, but all are beholden to others who are even more powerful than they are. So be very, very careful. I will be praying for you" and"

Kneeling at his *prieu dieu*, he clasped his hands in silent prayer.

✛ ✛ ✛

As Rosso approached St Peters, he was stunned again by its awesome majesty and the skill of the mortal hands that had crafted such a massive structure, with its statues and pillars. Workmen were busy everywhere, renovating the building that had fallen into disrepair whilst the Pope was living far away in France. The Popes and the Emperors had settled their differences and the "real" Pope was back in Rome, safely ensconced in his Papal palace.

The princes of the Church mingled in cloistered quietness in a building to one side of St Peter's, and that is where Rosso was to meet with Cardinal Visconti. His heart raced at the very thought of the Visconti name.

A guard stopped him, demanding to know his business before dispatching a messenger to the Cardinal's office for confirmation. Rosso waited, soaking up his surroundings. He could not believe that he, a runaway butcher's boy from the dregs of Venice, should be standing here at the centre of such power, at the very heart of the Christian empire.

When some of the leaders of the church walked past, in crimson splendor, Rosso was intrigued by the youth of one in the group.

"Surely he's far too young to be a Cardinal! How old is he?" he asked the guard.

"Not much older than you I reckon," the Swiss mercenary answered. "But most of em are pretty old."

Rosso watched the young Cardinal move silently down the corridor, his silken robes sweeping the floor behind him, as if to remove any trace of his youthful footsteps.

A taller man in priestly garb walked next to this young Cardinal, who leaned in close to his master, as a teacher would a student.

"The other un—*he's* the real power there," the guard added. "He's a Borgia, and some says that one day e'll get the top job ere."

The guard picked up a couple of walnuts, cracked them in his hand, and offered one to Rosso. As Rosso lifted the welcome gift to his lips, a beautiful young lady appeared, her leather-soled feet making light tapping sounds on the marbled floor as she gained ground on the two men ahead of her. As a whiff of sweet perfume swam before Rosso's nose, he thought she was the most beautiful woman he'd ever seen.

"And that there lady is the Pope's daughter…" the guard mumbled, "in an *unofficial* sort of way, if you get my drift."

"The Pope's *daughter!*" Rosso whispered, remembering all the rumors about the Popes' and Cardinals' private lives, but all the same, he could not take his eyes off the beauty before him.

"Well, they do say that priests should be celibate, but maybe abstinence is the one temptation that some of them can't resist."

The arrival of Cardinal Visconti's secretary interrupted his line of thought. The secretary was a fat man with a blubbery face, who proffered a blubbery grip when shaking hands. His jet black eyes rested uneasily in his rotund face, and though his mouth offered obsequious gratitude for Rosso having answered the Cardinal's call, the rest of his blubbered body spoke of animal instinct and rat-like cunning.

Rosso followed him along the frescoed corridors until they came to one that appeared to be shrouded in velvet silence. The secretary knocked at the door and waited.

"He won't keep you waiting long," he said with a wheezy voice "He's got a visitor with him who wants to meet you too."

He turned and went to a small desk beside the door, oozed his oversized mass behind it, and sat in reflected glory.

Rosso waited. After a while, the door opened without a sound and a voice called out.

"Brother Rosso?"

Cardinal Visconti stood there in a simple soutane while sporting a simple smile. Rosso leaned and kissed the Cardinal's ring, muttering, "Your Eminence."

The Cardinal led him into a room with an incredibly high ceiling, painted with glorious scenes from the Old Testament. The paneled walls were lined with shelves, stacked with tomes and parchments. A huge teak desk, polished to a stygian blackness, sat at the centre of the room, mirroring the glories of the vault above. To one side, there were two high-backed chairs that faced an open fire, heaped high with spitting logs and glowing embers.

"I'm so glad you could come," his Eminence nodded, indicating that Rosso should join him by the fireside. "No need to be afraid. I have but a simple task for you—one that demands a certain amount of discomfort. More importantly, it does demand that the person fulfilling the task should be able to speak French fluently. Unfortunately, in the present climate, it's a little challenging to find someone whom we can—how can I put this in Christian terms—someone whom we can trust."

He let the statement hang in the air. The suspense felt like a noose, tightening around the young monk's neck. Rosso blushed out of innocence, but he said nothing.

"I've learned a little from your Superiors, but perhaps you could tell me more about yourself, Brother Rosso."

The Cardinal leaned back in his chair, tapping his fingers together, staring into the embers of the fire

Rosso told his story to Cardinal Visconti, but he skipped the part Agnes played in his rescue and renewal. Perhaps it was to protect the one part of his life that was the most precious to him, or maybe it was because he was embarrassed about it. He kept his time spent with Agnes locked safely away in his memory.

Visconti remained silent after Rosso completed his story, still eyeing the embers. Rosso could not imagine or read whatever the man was thinking. The Cardinal stirred only after he had come to a decision.

"You're either a very simple, honest monk, or you're more intelligent and devious than your story would suggest."

He reached for a bell and rang it twice. The secretary entered the room instantly, wrapped in obsequious humility, yet his feral eyes roamed the room, seeking out the smallest bit of information that he could store away for future benefit.

"Ah, Giuda," the Cardinal said. "Ask my other guest to join us now."

Retreating from the room backwards, Giuda squeezed his bulky form through the partly-opened door and disappeared. The deep silence in the room returned whilst they waited, but it was soon fractured by a sharp rap on the door and the appearance of a tall, lean man in a Cardinal's cape.

"Your Eminence," Visconti called. "I'm so glad you could join us at such short notice."

Rreaching out to his fellow prince, they embraced each other in a symbolic, but hardly friendly fashion.

"This is the young man I was telling you about."

He turned toward Rosso.

"Brother Rosso this is our French cousin, Cardinal Villeprieux."

Rosso's face must have reflected the stunning effect the name had on his emotions, because Visconti smiled in a knowing way.

"I *though*t the name might surprise you. You see, it appears that *someone* bearing your family name has already shared some—how can I put it politely—*adventures* with Brother Rosso."

If the Frenchman had any inkling of any such person, there was not one iota of confirmation in his face or in his demeanor.

"It's an unusual name, I agree," he said with a wry smile, "and even more rare on *this* side of the Alps, but I know nothing of any such man. Shall we get down to business?

I'd like to interview this young man in private, if I could, your Eminence?"

"Certainly you may. Please accept the hospitality of my humble chambers," Visconti answered. "I have business to attend to, which will occupy me for some time. Just let Giuda know when you wish to leave, and he will call your guard for you."

They embraced again, like two actors on a stage. Before leaving, Cardinal Visconti scanned the room to make sure there was nothing left on display for prying eyes.

Cardinal Villeprieux sat in the vacated chair by the fire and ordered Rosso to sit next to him.

"We shall speak in French, because although we may be next to the house of God, sometimes I think the devil himself must live in this building. Now tell me of yourself and your travels, Brother Rosso, but take your time and omit nothing. I'd particularly like to know more of this man who called himself Villeprieux too."

He closed his eyes, leaning his head against the back of the chair, appearing to be fast asleep.

When Rosso finished, Cardinal Villeprieux opened his eyes.

"You speak perfect Parisian French, monsieur. You have had a difficult life and experienced strange times, and yet you seem untroubled by the suffering you've been through."

"I've been blessed by the people I've met since I left home, your Eminence. Given that I could have met less wholesome people, I thank God that he put those good people in my path—who carried me when I could not walk."

"Well said, young man. We live in a mystery, surrounded by suffering, and yet somehow kindness and love survive. But I would have you tell me more about this young Villeprieux. Perhaps I may know something of him, after all."

Rosso proceeded to tell the Cardinal as much as he could remember about his dear friend. He found himself warming to the odd, aesthetic priest in his crimson costume—a costume worn as the symbol of his mission, and yet a costume that shielded his secrets from prying eyes.

The Cardinal smiled after Rosso gave his account of his friend, Villeprieux.

"It sounds as if you loved this Frenchman very much."

"He saved my life and taught me so much, and yet he had no cause to. I could find no fault in him, and yes—he meant so much to me as a very dear friend. Not knowing whether he is dead or whether he was taken hostage occupies much of my thoughts and prayers."

For some strange reason, the words that Agnes had spoken to him in the cabin came to him—"be wary of this man" was all that she had said—and those words caused him to falter for a moment. The Cardinal continued in Italian,

"Sadly, I shall never meet this young man, even though he sounds a most intriguing person. However, from what you tell me, he has no connections to my family in any way."

He changed the subject.

"If you should be asked to come to Paris, then I'd like you to visit me and tell me more about how your studies progress here in Rome. But now I must leave."

Rising from his chair he extended his hand so that Rosso could kiss his ring. Reaching out, Rosso clasped the tips of the Cardinal's fingers and placed his lips on the cold gold of his princely seal. As he moved back, Cardinal Villeprieux gripped his hand and whispered, in his native French.

"Be wary of your friends, young man," he warned, glancing around at the four walls, "And be even more wary of what you say within these four walls too."

Then he dismissed him.

Rosso went to the door and let himself out just as Giuda was rising from behind his desk. Rosso didn't notice the scrap of paper that the man had crushed in the palm of his hand, and he didn't notice when Giuda bumped shoulders with a colorful courtier and palmed that crushed note into the other's hand as he led the young monk from the Vatican palace. And Rosso certainly didn't notice the colorful courtier pause to read the note, before turning on his heel to follow the young monk through the shadows of the city of Rome.

✢ ✢ ✢

When Rosso returned to the Friary, he sought out Brother Bart to inform him of the day's intriguing events.

"It was amazing," Rosso said. "I got a message to go to the Vatican palace. When I got there, I was asked to repeat my life story, first in Italian, and then in French. Then I was told that I shouldn't talk to anyone, because you can't trust anyone—especially anyone inside the Vatican."

He scratched the itchy stubble on the vault of his skull, giving Brother Bart a wry smile. The account didn't appear to trouble the aged monk as he moved around the small room, rearranging papers and books and opening his window. As a cockroach scurried across his desk, the old monk quick reflexes that allowed him to crush the vagrant insect amazed Rosso.

"Good shot, Bart!" escaped his lips before he could control his tongue. The old monk scrapped the flattened remains off the desk with a piece of paper and tossed it out the window.

"If only we could do the same with the noxious creatures that exist within our holy church," Bart said in a surprising moment of honesty. "These are difficult times, brother Rosso. Men of power, princes of the realms, kings, and others of great wealth are all plotting to increase their sway over the others, to get more power or to consolidate what they already have with new alliances. There's so much going on that we'll never hear of. Many men and women are bought and traded—like commodities by these people for such purposes. I suspect that you've flown close to their web for no other reason than that you're an innocent and you speak another language."

He screwed a piece of paper up and crushed it between both hands before tossing it in the litter bin beneath the desk.

"When we first met, I counseled you to listen to your our heart, and I repeat that counsel today. Don't be swayed by power, money, status or thoughts of fame. Be your own master, and our Master, who sees everything will not abandon you."

Holding Rosso by the shoulders, a small stream of tears following the deep creases below his red rimmed eyes, he concluded.

"I think you should go to your room and sit quietly for a few hours until your mind settles and you can find some peace again."

"Thank you, Brother Bart," Rosso replied "that sounds like a very good idea." Clasping his hands in billowing sleeves of his habit, he walked through the cloisters nodded, appreciative, on his way to meditate in splendid isolation and the healing embrace of silence for the rest of the day.

12

A LITTLE GIRL LOST

EACH WEEK in the Piazza near the Abbey, a small market was held, such as happens in many piazzas and market squares in villages, towns, and cities around the land.

"Do you know who came up with the idea for a market?" the old farmer asked to no one in particular, whilst jabbing his finger in the direction of the colorful stalls in front of him. "Well I reckon it was a farmer who maybe had too many olives one year but didn't have the price for a jug of wine. So what does he do? He takes a basket of his olives into the center of the town and cries out loud that, *If anyone is interested, I've got some really magnificent olives for sale.* Whereupon, the draper's wife, who had run out of ideas of how to make pasta more appealing to her hungry husband's savage stomach, sees the man with his olives thinks to herself, *Now, if I brined those olives for a few days and then added them to some tomatoes and poured that over the pasta, with maybe a few capers and peppers to add to the flavor..."*

The old farmer paused and ruminated on his great thesis, sucking in a great deal of cool air and blowing out a great deal of hot air, before continuing.

"Such thoughts may never have happened, but if they did and she bought the farmer's olives, then more than likely, she went home pretty happy with her prize, and no doubt her old man's stomach was pretty happy with the food she served up too. And the farmer who sold them olives would have been delighted and gone home happily to his wife, who would no doubt find several ways of spending his new found wealth."

After pausing for effect, he reached the crescendo of his great insight.

"Now, should the draper's wife tell of such an enterprise to her fellows after worship on a Sunday, and should the farmer tell his fellow imbibers at his local tavern on a Monday, then word would quickly spread."

Stopping to look at the small crowd that had gathered around him, he concluded.

"And perhaps that's how it all began."

Beaming at his friends, he soaked up the laughter and backslaps and graciously accepted several offers to visit the local taverna to have a "small glass of something, *cos all that talkin gives me an awful dry throat.*

As the small crowd dispersed, Rosso ambled down the lane and into the piazza, at the market. It was near his monastery and made up of several colorful merchants' stalls and foul-smelling animal pens. Five cobbled laneways led the human and vegetable cargo into the small square, which echoed the squeals of animals and calls of vegetable and cloth vendors.

There were forge doors in the square, where horses were husbanded by the sweaty smithy. This man's powerful hands could brandish a massive hammer and yet handle any animal with the lightest touch. Marco, the blacksmith, stood tall amongst his fellows. His reputation came from his physical strength as well as his wisdom of mind.

When a vagabond child tried to steal one of his horseshoes on display outside his forge, he picked the child up by the scruff of his shirt, letting his legs dangle, suspended in mid-air, until his small lungs ran out of breath. Then he looked him in the eye, searching for that glimpse of true humanity, and once he recognized it, he let him down, and with a firm shove, he pushed him back into the maelstrom that made up his unfettered life.

He never said a word to any of the many who found themselves suspended in mid animation. He just wanted to check that there was a spark of hope there, and once he was satisfied, he let them go. Marco never held onto any child or felt the need to check them further—just that one searching look was all he—and they needed.

Rosso walked past Marco's forge into the square to get some vegetables for the Abbey. Getting vegetables was the job for the most junior of the brothers, and though it marked him as a novice, he enjoyed being out among the people and hearing the normal sounds of life.

"Silent prayer," he mused to himself, "may be a wonderful way to reflect on what's happening, and to make a word picture that God might perhaps admire, but I really miss the smells, the sights, and the sounds."

He sucked in a full lungful of market air.

"Decisions, decisions," he said to himself, as he watched people go about their business, or gossip about the business of other people.

Many came to the market to stock up on provisions, and they went about their tasks with a grim determination, but there were others who came because markets meant people—and Romans loved to talk! Nearby, there was a group of three men who could be discussing the latest edict to come from the Pope himself. Or perhaps they were elucidating on the merits of the latest Da Vinci invention. Or more likely, it was how the local landowners had managed again to gain another monopoly over the city's grain supply.

Rosso enjoyed watching their animated bodies keep time to the musical sound of their voices. Eyes that were slits conspiracy became sudden lakes of wonder. The subject of their conversation was going around another time when a young woman approached. She had an enchanted air about her, not only because of her blond hair and blue eyes, which are unusual for Romans, but because of the quiet aura that moved with her.

Wherever she lingered, she greeted the owner with respect, always inquiring after their families, and when she moved on, she seemed to leave an unseen scent of kindness in her wake, a brief blessing amidst the noise and turmoil of the usual market mood.

Rosso watched her as she headed for the forge with the things she had bought. As she got closer, Marco stilled his hammer, his eyes and his heart focusing on the approaching lady. She stopped right in front of him, saying nothing. She merely inclined her head and held out her hand to him. His powerful hand reached out and gently held her fingertips, whilst all around them the world hurtled about its frenetic business.

Rosso felt a flash of guilt for having been witness to such a moment of perfect intimacy and turned his head away. When he looked back, the door to the house from the forge was closing and the clank of Marco's hammer rang out around the market, singing over the cacophony of people, cattle, breezes and bells.

Cheese! he thought to himself. Which cheese did the Abbot say he'd like? He gathered his thoughts and headed for the great rounds of cheese that lay on the stall nearby. He knew the stallholder well, and he was confident the man would be able to remember which cheese the Abbot liked best, saving himself from another rebuke for not being able to follow simple Monastic orders!

As he crossed into the square, he was nearly hit by a decrepit carrier's cart, rumbling past at a decidedly un-market like pace. The heavily-laden cart was driven by a feral-looking fellow, driving his donkey hard, constantly looking over his shoulder, as if he was being followed by the bailiff or the devil himself. With the reins in one hand

and the whip in the other, he fought a losing battle to keep his cap from falling down over his eyes.

Soon he was gone out of the piazza, and Rosso moved his eyes and his mind from what he had just seen and on to what he must do.

13
CHEESE

HE WAS STANDING by the stall, whilst a lady of generous proportions explained, in a very longwinded way, how she had eaten a particular cheese at her nephew's wedding only last month in a small town ten miles away. She said it was delicious cheese, and she hoped perhaps the owner of the stall might be able to suggest what type of cheese it might have been.

As she went on, Rosso felt a tug at his habit. Thinking that he might have caught it on something, he stepped away from the source of the tug. Then it was there again, but it was accompanied by the sound of a little voice.

"Excuse me please," the voice piped up at him in a pleasant, pleading tune. "Please, have you seen my uncle?"

Even though he was still young and ignorant of the many ways of the world, Rosso always had time for children. Perhaps it was the memory of his little sister who had so adored him, but whenever he met a needy child, he always descended to that little person's level, which in the eyes of the wise, exalted him to a higher level. So he squatted down to look at the bedraggled bundle of rags that had summoned his attention.

What he saw was a dirty, bleary-eyed, tangle-haired, bruised-armed, wasted little creature, whose clothes suggested they had been borrowed from an infant scarecrow. He saw the neglect in her outer clothing, but he sensed something more in her dark brown eyes. It was the look of someone who really was lost, and not just physically, but emotionally and spiritually as well. Rosso held her by both arms.

"What does your uncle look like, little girl?"

"He was driving our cart, and he asked me to give a message to a man in a shop, but the man in the shop said he'd never heard of my uncle. When I got back, he'd disappeared," she explained as the first tears swelled from her eyes to run down her grimy face.

"Was it an old cart with lots of old stuff piled high on it?" Rosso asked in a soft voice.

She nodded her head as more tears descended, accompanied by an increasing, yet silent heaving of her shoulders.

Rosso held the little girl close in his arms whilst her little heart beat as fast as a frightened sparrow. When the heaving settled and the tears slowed their terrible streams, he wiped her eyes and moved her away from the crowd in order to enquire more of her.

Whilst they were sitting by the edge of the piazza, the sun warmed Rosso's back, and the child, exhausted by hunger and drained by her desperate emotions, fell asleep. All the while, life went on around them. The penned pigs made their grunting indignation known to everyone by fouling the cobbled streets, and the sounds of human voices—some bargaining, some bemoaning, and one even singing—joined together to create a fresco of sound around the square. But above it all, with its rhythmic "clang, clang, clang," was the sound of iron on iron from Marco's forge.

A shadow fell over Rosso in the willowy form of Pietro.

"There's no doubt about it, Rosso, what the good St Francis did with animals, you seem to be able to do with children," he said with a smile whilst leaning on his stick.

On that day, his pain was such that walking any distance was a true penance for him, but he endured it all with a quiet resignation.

"I haven't seen you for a few days, young monk. How's the Dom getting on?"

He drew his beads from his pocket and turned them in his hand at a furious pace.

"He's going well, and Gian's children love him," Rosso replied.

"And who's this you've got with you today? She looks exhausted, the poor mite," Pietro commented, forgetting his own pain.

"I literally tripped over her," Rosso answered. "But look at her. It makes me savage, seeing how neglected she is, and if I'm not wrong, she has been badly abused too."

His old friend gripped him by the shoulder to help him relax. Taking a deep breath, Rosso continued.

"From what she's told me and from what I saw with my own eyes, my guess is that whoever she's been living with has abandoned her in the piazza. If that's the case, then I'm afraid she's destined to join all those other lost and forgotten kids who will either die young or be damaged for life. You'd know better than most, Pietro, that's not much of a choice for a little girl."

The thought of his own bleak childhood reached from his dark memory like a newly opened wound. A silence enveloped the two men as they grieved for the suffering child before their eyes, and yet the world went its noisy way around them. All this time, the "clang, clang, clang" nagged at Rosso's mind, like a missing clue in a mystery.

"Well, I don't think the Abbot would be too pleased if you take her to the monastery. Remember what happened the last time you asked?"

If it hadn't been so very sad, it would have been farcical to recount. Rosso had found a beaten boy on the streets. The child was unconscious—not just from his injuries, but from the deprivation he had suffered during his short life.

How could they call Rome a Christian place, when the boy's father, an alcoholic sailor—no longer fit go to sea, had indentured his own son to clean out the bilges of cargo ships recently returned from Egypt? The father advocated that, because the boy was so small, he could get into tight spaces where a normal person couldn't—the sort of places where rats and debris accumulate; the sorts of unpleasant detritus that might prove a threat to the ship!

That poor blighted child had stuck it out for a few months, but when summer came and the heat in those hell holes was unbearable, he ran away to Brother Rosso, claiming sanctuary from the Church. And what did the Abbot say? What did this exulted follower of Christ, who said, "Let the little children come unto me," say to Brother Rosso?

"A boy needs his father. We shouldn't interfere."

The words hit Rosso like a rock, falling on a little coffin lid.

As he caressed the little girl's face, Rosso shook his head at the warped morality of the Church, pulling the ragged bundle of a child closer to his chest. He looked up, shaking his head toward Pietro

"Did you hear that?" he asked.

"I didn't hear anything," his friend answered, turning to seek the unheard sound.

"It's *stopped*!" Rosso indicated.

"Forgive me, my friend, but *what's* stopped?"

"Marco's hammer," Rosso answered. "I think there might be someone who can help, and I'd really appreciate it if you could come with me, because I think you know them better than I do."

They headed off across the square to the forge where, Marco had laid down his hammer and had begun the job of damping down the forge fire.

"For a former soldier, you give a new meaning to bearing arms, Brother Rosso," Marco laughed as he eyed the bundle of rags the young man carried, "And I can see a couple of very thin legs too."

"There's nothing to her. She's as light as a little feather," Rosso said in a soft voice, brushing the stray hairs away from her eyes.

As he looked down at her, he remembered how he'd held his little sister when she was so sick with the fever. He looked up.

"Pietro and I have been thinking of what we can do to help the poor mite. My recent track record at trying to help these children hasn't been too good of late," the young monk said, looking down at the blue pools surrounding her sunken eyes.

Meanwhile, Marco had opened the door to the house and beckoned them all through whilst calling out.

"Laura, can you come down a moment? We need a mother's common sense down here."

There were movements from the first floor, followed by a slight creaking on the wooden stairs, and then Laura arrived. She went straight to her husband's side and they twined their little fingers together as they looked at Rosso and his light burden.

"Greetings, Brother Rosso, and welcome dear Pietro," she said, giving them both a light kiss on both cheeks. "Where did you find this poor creature, Rosso? Is she sick? Bring her into the kitchen where there's warmth, and I'll see if I can get her to eat something."

Giving Marco's finger a final loving squeeze, she led them into the kitchen. The kitchen was the heart of the house, and everything that happened in the house beat out from that simple room. Laura's kitchen was like the forge that helped form Marco's wrought iron creations—except her fire forged the hearts and minds of all who visited.

Her fire was simple, well-tended and overhung with all the usual implements to be found in such a domestic environment. Next to the fire, there was a little nook that was home to an upturned crate—a favorite spot for little children when they came in from playing on a cold winter's days. The large deal table was scrubbed clean, and there were were clean, empty dishes on it, suggesting that the next meal time was not far off.

There was a sideboard against one wall, decked out with mementoes from the passing parade that marked the passage of time in a happy family home. Besides the door to the forge, there was one that led to the rest of the house, and there was one that led outside. Through this outside door, sounds slowly swelled and then burst through, in the form of the three young children.

"There are monsters in the backyard, thousands of them! And Sara says that they're going to get us!" the first scamp panted, his bright eyes glittering with excitement.

"Yes, and I've killed millions of them with my bow so far, but I've run out of arrows and need to hide," the second scamp added, his dark hair standing straight up on his animated head.

Finally, Sara walked through the door and flopped down on the bench next to the kitchen table. She was about to comment on the monsters when a worried frown creased her young forehead.

"Who's that little child, Mamma?"

Laura explained to the children what little she knew of the poor child as she poured them each a mug of water from a stone jug. Turning to look at the poor child, she spoke to her children.

"I think you've made enough noise to awaken the dead."

At that moment, the little child opened her eyes, staring about the room. When she saw Marco, she shrank back into Rosso's chest, but when she looked up and saw Rosso's stubbly face, she whimpered and leapt from his lap and into the welcoming arms of Laura. From there, she glanced anxiously around, her eyes falling on the faces of the children who watched in bemused fascination.

These blessed children had never experienced suffering or want in their lives, and they thought that the little ragamuffin was like them. Then the child's eyes rested on Pietro, and he held her gaze with his soft eyes. She didn't retreat from them, but the very sight of Marco and Rosso made her retreat further into Laura's embrace.

"I don't think she likes men very much," Laura surmised.

"Then why did she pull at my clothes?" Rosso asked, giving Laura a nonplussed look.

"Probably because you're young and dress up like a woman," said Pietro with a grin, dispelling the tension in the room as the children giggled at Rosso's discomfort.

"The big question is, what do we do with her now?" Marco asked.

"She can have my bed, Mama," Sara said. "And I can have the boys' bed, and they can sleep on the floor," she said with a wink to Pietro.

Her suggestion led to instant agony for her two younger brothers, but before they had worked through the cunning trap laid by their senior sister, Laura came to their rescue.

"Of course, she must stay here until we find out more about her story, but first things first—food, bath, and then bed. It's getting late for young children."

As she said that, she nodded at Marco who held out his arms towards the poor child to welcome her, but she shrank away from him again. The powerful smith winced as if he'd been physically hurt by an unseen stab.

"Why don't we men go outside and leave Laura to do what needs to be done?" Pietro suggested as he headed for his stick and then the forge. The young child followed the men with her eyes and then surrendered herself to the kind benevolence of the gentle mother.

Gathered around the damped down fire in the forge, the men began to discuss where they should begin to make inquiries when the Abbey bell began to chime.

"Oh dear God, cabbages and cheese!" cried Rosso, "I have to get back to the market and get those provisions, or I'll be skinned alive! I'll see you tomorrow, and we'll talk more then."

"That's what I love about our religion, Marco," Pietro chuckled, "—cabbages, cheese and being skinned alive— there's something in it for *everyone!*"

Pietro retrieved the beads and began turning them through his fingers slowly, indicating that he wasn't in any hurry—and he wasn't in danger of being skinned alive!

"Aye," replied the thoughtful smith, "But *suffer little children to come unto me*. Isn't that's what it says in the good book? But what do we do when the poor mites won't come anywhere near us, let alone try to help them?"

He gazed into the coals, prodding them with his workaday poker, whilst Pietro quietly worked his beads.

"There's no real rush to get any answers. The first thing is to get that young one right, because she's not right at the moment, and it grieves my heart to see her so," Marco said.

"I agree," Pietro nodded. "I don't get around as much as most, but it's funny how often news seems to come to me. So I'll keep my eyes and ears open to see who she might be and where she's come from."

With that he put his beads back in his pocket and bade his companion farewell.

Marco retreated into the kitchen, which was empty. A bath tub stood in front of the fire, which Laura was filling with the water, heated in kettles from over the fire.

"Where are the children?" he asked with a bewildered expression.

"Well," said Laura with a smile, "she was sitting on my lap like a scared rabbit after you men had gone out, and then the two boys started acting like goats, and that made her smile. And you'd be so proud of your daughter. She just came over to her and asked if she wanted to go outside and play. Down she pops, and the two of them walk out the door, hand in hand, as if they've been friends for life. And by the way, her name's Clare."

"How on Earth did you find that out so quickly?" Marco asked.

"Simple really, and I don't know why someone didn't think of it before. Sara asked her what her name was as they were going outside, and she said it was Clare."

Soon there were sounds of happy children doing what happy children do best—playing, having adventures, making up games and talking! But Clare was weak and she was hungry, so Sara led her little tribe back into the kitchen, where her mother took charge. Sitting to eat together had never stopped the children from talking sixteen to the dozen, and although Clare rarely entered the debates, her face was more animated than it had been when she had first arrived.

But when Marco approached the children, she froze and retreated into herself.

"Poor mite," he groaned. "It breaks my heart to see her like this. What do you think I should do?"

"Just be yourself," Laura said, "but give Clare some space and give her some time. She'll come around. You'll see. When she sees how much you love your family, she'll come to accept you too."

Later on, when the light began to fail and the lamp in the kitchen had been lit, it was time to think of bed. Sara gave Clare one of her old nightgowns, and the children climbed the stairs to the loft, above the forge. Then the boys went to one bed and the girls went to the other, top-to-toe fashion.

Marco led them in family prayers, with each child saying a separate prayer out loud. From past experience, it was often a serious, solemn time, with admissions like, "Dear God, it was an accident that the widow got broken…" At other times, the session turned into one of those silly giggling periods when it was best to finish early and let God savor one of the few happy moments of His long, challenging day.

That night, each of the children spoke of how happy they were that Clare was with them and about all the adventures they were going to have. In a gentle voice, Marco asked if Clare wanted to say a small prayer, but she shrank back at his words and said nothing. Laura hugged all the children, bidding them goodnight, but Marco hugged only his own. As they went downstairs, Laura gave Marco her little finger again, and he felt at peace.

When they reached the kitchen, they tidied away the remains of the family meal and lit candles in preparation for going to bed.

"I saw something strange today," Laura said over her shoulder as she washed the dishes.

"And what, pray, was that, my little foster mother?" Marco teased.

"Well," she said, ignoring his jibe, "when I was washing little Clare's hair today, her head began to bleed. Now, I know the poor mite has had a terrible life so far, but it seemed strange that she should bleed from her head. So I had a closer look and discovered a red birthmark at the back of her head, but it's covered by her lovely hair. She said it often bleeds from there but it stops if you press on it for long enough. She seemed so matter-of-fact about it all. But the strangest part of it is the shape. When you clear her hair away, you'd almost imagine you're looking at a red butterfly."

She paused to reflect on what she had just said.

"Yes, that's it," she continued. "It's odd that something that seemingly looks so beautiful could be so ugly too."

She glanced over to find that Marco was staring at her with a big smile of his face.

"Now tell me, Mr. Muscles, what's so funny in what I just said?"

"You're the most amazing woman I have met, or will ever meet," he said, putting his arms around her waist. Pulling her close, he whispered, "I love you so much, and I'm so happy you're the mother of our children. I think that perhaps little Clare was sent here—not only for our benefit, but to remind us of how very lucky we are."

He held her tight against him, and picking up the candle, he whispered.

"Let's go to bed."

14

A CALL FROM THE CARDINAL

AS THE WEEKS went by, Clare became a natural part of Marco and Laura's family, although she was still uncertain about Marco and feared physical contact with him. However, one evening, after they finished their family prayers and Marco had hugged his children—as he was about to leave the room, he heard a soft, little voice.

"Me too, please…"

Looking back in the light of the golden candle, he saw the glistening eyes of Clare, sitting up in bed next to Sara, with outstretched arms.

When he went downstairs a few minutes later, he was still wiping the tears from his eyes, but his face ached with trembling joy.

"What happened," Laura asked, staring in amazement at her normally stoic husband.

Yet when he told her had happened, they both embraced and rocked gently in each other's arms.

During those weeks, Pietro and Rosso were constant visitors, and the children were delighted, especially when they brought small gifts. Pietro had discovered more about Clare's history: a servant girl delivered her as a baby to a convent for foundlings; the servant told the Sisters that the mother was someone in service, who died in childbirth; when the Sisters asked who the father was, the servant was less forthcoming, saying that she thought he was French, but more than that, she knew nothing, or at least would say nothing.

The servant was certain, however, that no one wanted the infant and asked the Sisters to take her. Otherwise, she would be left to die somewhere in the streets. Naturally, the Sisters took her in and cared for her. *What was one extra mouth amongst so many?* Because they had so many mouths to feed, they were always delighted when any of the babies were taken for adoption.

According to the Sister who Pietro spoke to, she remembered that particular child, because it was her own sister who adopted her. This older sister had been trying for several years to have a baby, and she and her husband had begun to despair of having a child of their own. The Sister told the couple that she would find a child for them, and for some reason, she chose Clare.

Sadly, the sister had died some years later, and the husband remarried. His new wife had given him a son, which for Clare meant that they had no need of the young girl anymore.

"They were the wife's very words," Pietro emphasized. "They had no need of her any more. How can you say that about an innocent child?" he said, looking toward Marco, Laura and Rosso.

It seemed that the nun had lost contact with Clare, but she understood that a cousin of the adopted father had taken her to where she and her husband lived at some small, run-down taverna in the country. After that, the Sister knew nothing else.

"Many of the locals know of that particular taverna and of the unpleasant couple who used to run it. And I did hear from some traveling people that there was a small child involved, and by all reports, she was sorely used. Just recently, the woman had died—stabbed in some domestic brawl, so the rumor goes, and the taverna was shut down. Nobody has seen anything of the owner or the little girl for some weeks now. But the story seems to fit, and her recent arrival would appear to confirm the story too."

"Well, mystery or no mystery," Laura concluded, "Frenchman or no Frenchman, she stays here until someone can convince me that there's somewhere better for her to go."

Though she spoke the words in a soft tone, there was steel in her voice.

"Thanks for that, Pietro," Marco added. "It's starting to become a little clearer now, and I know I speak for Laura when I say that we'd be so happy to keep her here in our little family, if she'll have us. She'll be safe and much loved with us."

"Laura and Marco—you inspire me" Rosso beamed, and realizing the hour it was, he rose.

"However, I'm sorry to break up the company, but strange as it may seem, the Abbot is not totally impressed with his red-headed novice at the moment, so I must return to the monastery to at least *pretend* to be a good monk."

After embracing each one in turn, he left the forge.

When he reached the Friary, a voice that reminded him of the creaking beams of ship's hulk called out from the porters lodge.

"The Abbot wants to see you. Now!" and with that, the gatekeeper slammed the small wooden window in his face.

And God bless you too, thought Rosso as he straightened his habit, tucked his hands in his sleeve and marched, very monk-like, to the Abbot's office.

"Enter," was the response to his knock.

"Ah, Brother Rosso—have you made a decision on your final vows? We don't want to rush you in any way," the Abbot said, his voice dripping with irony.

"Yes, Abbot, I have," Rosso answered. "I am at your convenience."

He averted his eyes in monastic obedience and humility. After a pause the Abbot responded.

"Well, apparently it's *not* convenient."

Rosso looked up in confusion as the older man continued.

"It's not convenient because Cardinal Visconti wants to see you straight away at the Vatican. It seems the monastery's petty rituals will have to wait until you can find time to fit us into your busy *schedule*, Brother Rosso."

Rosso's mind was in turmoil, but he was given no time to say anything before the Abbot dismissed him. Rosso had no things in his room to collect, so he did not need to stop there. He made straight for the Vatican and his meeting with Cardinal Visconti, announcing himself to the guards, who dispatched a messenger to the Cardinal's secretary.

Soon, Giuda came down the long corridor to escort Rosso into the Cardinal's presence.

"I trust you and your friends are well?" Guida asked.

Remembering Brother Bart's words, Rosso merely nodded in response and kept walking.

When they reached the Cardinal's room, Giuda knocked and entered, closing the door behind him. He reappeared a few minutes later to usher Rosso into the Cardinal's presence.

"Brother Rosso, I'm so glad you could make it," the prince of the Church said with feigned politeness. "I have a special *ministry* for you," he said, pausing over the word "ministry," as if it were a pleasant surprise to find such a word for such an endeavor. "You'll immediately make plans to travel to France to meet with Cardinal Villeprieux, who'll give you further instructions when you get there."

Moving closer to Rosso, he continued.

"It might be wise to carefully consider the route you take, as there are others who may take a special interest in you—*if they knew who sent you and to whom you were going to meet*."

The Cardinal did not elaborate on what he meant, but the threat implicit in his words hit their mark, giving Rosso the sudden impression that he had just landed on the sticky part of a spider's web, whilst he had no idea who were the masters of the web.

"Any questions?" Visconti asked in a voice that expected there to be none.

"Does immediately mean *now*?" Rosso asked.

"That would be correct," the Cardinal replied as he rang his bell.

As usual, the door opened right away and Giuda appeared.

"Do give Brother Rosso the purse I prepared for his expenses. That's all, Brother Rosso. God's blessing on you mission. You may leave now."

The Cardinal sat.

Bowing, Rosso turned and left in the wake of the bulky secretary.

"Off somewhere?" asked Giuda.

Rosso merely nodded his head, which was spinning, with the speed at which things seemed to be happening.

"Cat got your tongue," his guide said with a smile as he winked to a courier who just happened to be loitering nearby. "Well don't get lost before you get home. And be careful who you speak to," Giuda shouted, as Rosso began to cross the large square outside of St Peters.

As Giuda returned down those gilded corridors and back to his desk, his quivering cheeks hid his clenched teeth and shrouded his coal black eyes, but they couldn't conceal the contraction of the muscles that lifted the corners of his mouth into a rictus-like smile.

Rosso tried to think clearly as he crossed the Square. He had to get to Paris, or somewhere near Paris, where the Cardinal lived. But *how* to get there was the first challenge. He knew most of the country of northern Italy like he knew his own face, but to get to Paris was something beyond his comprehension.

Who can I ask? he thought to himself. He was not a Roman, but he knew that Rome was full of intrigue and spies. For all he knew, someone was following him even then, which made him pause and glance to the rear. Apart from the usual crowd, none seemed to look like foreign spies. Moving on, he made the decision to seek out Brother Julian, Gian, and the Dom, to see what they thought.

His path took him first to St Maria Maggiore, but one of the monks told him that Brother Julian was out, visiting the less fortunate in the community. Rosso suppressed a smile as he knew that it was Julian's code for visiting his brother, whilst at the same time, feeding his expanding girth. Rosso's heart lightened as he turned his face toward the family tavern, knowing that he would soon be amongst his dear friends.

Brother Julian and Gian were sitting, doing what Italians do so well—using their hands and faces whilst eating and speaking. Meanwhile, the Dom was playing peekaboo with one of the smaller children. The game involved covering his missing eye with his one hand and calling, "I can't *see* you. Where have you *gone?*" Then he would flip up the eye-patch over his good eye and say, "Peekaboo!" at which the players would laugh out loud.

"Do it again, Uncle Dom!"

And so the game continued. Rosso entered and sat to listen to the brothers' conversation.

"What brings you here today, Brother Rosso," Gian asked.

Rosso started to relate the extraordinary events of his day and of his planned trip to Paris, but had absolutely no idea how he was going to get there. The brothers listened whilst continuing to enjoy their meal. The Dom picked up most of the conversation between peels of childish laughter.

Finally, Julian looked at Gian.

"To my way of thinking brother, it seems to me that our friend here has little *choice* in the matter. He has been ordered to go to Paris by the Cardinal, so he must go. But there are parts of this mystery that are too dark and too deep for me to fathom, and that makes me very nervous for his safety."

He sipped on a glass of wine and waited for Gian to respond.

"I agree, brother. And if it's deep and dark to us, then you can be sure that there are some other unsavory characters who are watching and waiting to see what happens next. In which case, getting away from Rome without being noticed could create some challenges too."

Gian reached for his glass and sipped, washing down both food and thought.

The Dom lifted the child up onto his hip and came to sit at the table.

"Don't trust the French," was his sole contribution, but he said it in such a tone that no one spoke for a moment.

"All the Roman ports have spies," Gian explained. "So it's either south to Naples, or north to Milan, and then via Genoa to Marseilles."

"For me, brother, it has to be Milan—" Julian suggested, "the obvious route for a messenger is to travel from Rome. If you want to raise suspicion, then you go down to Naples and take a boat from there. Only a madman would take a message to Paris via Milan," he said, singing *Tra Lalla* in celebration of his inscrutable logic. "And of course, Milan has the undeniable benefit of being a Pilgrim route from the Holy Roman Empire, and one extra monk on that route shouldn't raise too many suspicions."

"One other thing," Rosso interjected, choosing his words carefully. "You've heard me talk about Clare?"

The men nodded as Rosso continued.

"Well, it seems that her father is French, and there's even a suggestion that he has noble blood. Do you think I should take her with me, or would that be placing too much risk on the young girl?"

Pausing for a moment, he continued.

"You do know that I would lay down my life for that child?"

The Dom reached out the stump of his arm and laid it on Rosso's hand.

"We know that, Rosso. We know that."

"One of the reasons I think that bringing her with me might help is because, I doubt if any spies will be looking for a monk and a little girl. And secondly, Laura told me in confidence—and may God forgive me for breaking that confidence— that Clare has a very distinctive birthmark on the back of her head, which I'm hoping will narrow down the search considerably."

"That's assuming that anyone else has the same birthmark," Gian said, dislodging a plank under Rosso's argument.

"You could be right," Rosso replied. "But from what Laura told me, this birthmark is really unusual, and I think it does give us some hope."

Brother Julian, who had been silent through the discussion, wiped his lips with a kerchief.

"I think that's the vital ingredient here, Brother Rosso—hope. If there's one thing that the little girl needs, it's hope. I know you'll love her as well as any brother possibly could, and if she wants to go, she couldn't be in safer hands. Why not go and ask her?"

Pouring glasses of wine for the Dom and Rosso, he proposed a toast.

"To hope!"

✢ ✢ ✢

Rosso was soon in the blacksmith's kitchen, recounting the tumultuous events of his day.

"I suppose the big question is, should I take Clare with me to see if we can find her father in Paris?"

Marco moved around the kitchen table and stood next to his wife.

"That's a big decision for a little girl, Laura replied. "Especially since she's been through so much, and she's just settling into a normal family routine."

She reached out to find her husband's hand. Just then, the door burst open and Sara and Clare tumbled in, full of the enthusiasm of childhood innocence. They stood giggling, looking from face to face, and then at each other as they realized they'd interrupted some grown-up talk.

"Sorry," Sara began, but her father interrupted.

"That's okay, darling. We were just talking about Clare, here."

Sara walked over to her father who embraced her, whilst Clare isolated herself in the doorway with her face falling.

"It's okay, my little one," Laura comforted, moving to her and sweeping her up.

"Rosso here has a story to tell you, and we'd like to hear what you think about it. So let's sit down at the table, have a drink of water, and listen to Brother Rosso."

It was as if the children had stumbled into a fairytale as Rosso paced around the kitchen, recounting what he knew about Clare, about what had happened to him, and about what Cardinal Visconti had instructed him to do. Then he paused, squatted next to Laura, and looked at Clare, who was enfolded in safe, strong arms.

"The real question, little sister, is will you come with me on my journey to Paris, where there might be a chance that we will find your real father? There are no guarantees, and it might be a difficult journey, but if we found your real father…"

His voice trailed off into the silence. Clare's big round eyes revealed nothing of the thoughts that were going through her mind at that moment. Then she slowly looked around at everyone, her eyes finally settling on Marco.

"I want a father like him," she said, pointing her finger at the erstwhile emotional blacksmith. "And if I can't find one like him, then I want to come back and live here."

Twisting around to look at Laura she smiled.

"Is that okay with you, Mamma?"

In that precious moment of insight by an innocent child, all were bound by the love that swirled around that wooden kitchen table. Marco was the first to break that spell.

"Everyone come here."

Holding out his brawny arms, he embraced wife, brother and children, his heart overflowing. Laura wiped her tears on her apron,

"If you two are off on a long journey, then you'll need some food to help you on your way."

Right away, she began preparing food for the trip. Emotional, Sara went over to Rosso and admonished him, in her role of eldest child and senior sister, to take good care of Clare. Rosso responded like the good novice that he was, suppressing an urge to smile.

Meanwhile, Clare still stood next to Marco.

"Will you let me hug you just once before you go," he asked.

Laura paused at her work, never turning, whilst Rosso and Sara looked at the little girl. Then, in the most natural of actions, as if she'd been doing it for all of her short life, she threw her arms around his neck and gave him a big squeeze. Marco swept her up into the air.

"I love you, my little one! I love you. Come home safely."

So it was that the tall red-headed monk, in his black habit, and his little companion, carrying her small sac, set off for Florence at dawn on the following day.

15

ON THE ROAD AGAIN

REMEMBERING HIS earlier travels, Rosso knew much of the terrain that he would cross after leaving the decay of Rome behind. As they crossed the flat marshy areas on their way to the cooler climate of the nearby hillside, Rosso thought that perhaps he had made a bad choice in taking the route. The flies were bad, but the mosquitoes were even worse, and the sun burned their faces in the shade-less land. Finally, they reached the slopes, and though the ascent of the steep hills was tiring, it was far better than being swarmed and bitten by the insects they'd left behind.

The weather cooled as they navigated the hills, the morning mists enshrouding the vast estates that clung to the great escarpments. There, they picked up a horse to help speed them on their way—and to put more distance between them and the prying eyes of their unknown and unseen pursuers.

As they moved away north, the hilly landscape was kept green by the mists, with fat sheep grazing beneath the olive groves. On that part of the journey, finding food was easy, as the locals were generous and hospitable. With little Clare by his side, it usually took less than five minutes before every the motherly instinct was aroused in each woman they met.

Though the people were country folks, they were used to travelers and were good judges of character. Although the sight of Rosso in his black habit was no real threat to them, any monk riding a horse did raise eyebrows.

"Strange to see folk like you on a fine horse like that," several farmers asked whilst running their hands over the flank of the beast.

"The Duke's her father, and she's been away visiting family in Rome. I'm her tutor, and it's my job to bring her home safely," Rosso answered with the smooth tongue of the mercenary he'd once been. Lying led to some temporary inner turmoil, but he concluded that as God knew everything, He would eventually sort it all out, and so he decided to leave such venial concerns to the Almighty!

As the days passed, so did the hills, slowly flattening out into the monotonous plains that seemed to go on for an eternity. Each morning, they set out, with Clare in front and Rosso behind. Sometimes, she would ask to slip down from their mount so that she could skip ahead and pick up objects that took her fancy along the path. Like all children, she had many questions, but both eventually tired, lapsing into silence, listening to the sounds of birds and breezes, and the hypnotic cadence of the clopping horse's hooves.

It seemed like weeks, crossing those endless plains, but the journey took them six days in the unseasonably dry weather. By the time they arrived in Milan, Clare's face had turned a glorious bronze, whilst Rosso merely developed more freckles and a red, peeling nose. The great walls of the city loomed ahead, with the towering presence of the Sforza stronghold, guarding the northern gate. Brother Julian gave instructions that they should make for the Church of Santa Maria Della Grazia, to the good Sisters at the convent next door, who would give them shelter for the night.

The church was close by the Sforza Castle, so even for two itinerant travelers from Rome, it didn't take long to find it. It was an unremarkable building in an unremarkable cobble-stoned street. They went in and lit a candle in thanksgiving for their safe journey.

Rosso knocked on the door of the convent next door and introduced himself to the gatekeeper. The Superior of the convent sent instructions for them to go to the refectory and get some food. She agreed to meet them later when she was free. As they were walking down the corridor, they met a bearded man, who appeared to be deep in thought.

"*Salve,*" Rosso said, the sound of his voice stirring the man from his reverie, invoking an exchange of greetings. At once, Rosso noticed the man's piercingly intense eyes.

"*Salve,*" the man replied. "Off for a bite to eat? You look like you need it? Have you been traveling for long?"

He stopped himself.

"I'm sorry. Too many questions, and too fast, but I've got a few things on my mind."

With that, he gave them a wan grin and continued down the passageway.

"Interesting looking fellow," said Rosso to Clare. "I wonder if he's a tradesman, or if he's just visiting like us?"

Just then, they reached the Refectory, where the Sisters ate and prayed their community prayers. At the gable end of the vast room, there was a breathtaking, magnificent mural on the wall, partly concealed by half erected-scaffolding. It was a depiction of Jesus and His disciples, eating their last meal together, although some of the faces were not complete.

"I see you've met our resident artist," the cook called out as she walked towards them from the other end of the room, carrying a tray of bread and wine. "He's a funny one. He's been at it for months and months. Sometimes, he just stands and looks at it for hours without even lifting a brush, and then he goes out again—just like he did just now."

Although there was a teasing tone to her voice, there was genuine admiration as she passed on that tidbit of information.

"What's his name?" Clare asked.

"He's called Leonardo," she replied. "He's been working for the Duke for some years now. But he doesn't only paint pictures. He's invented some amazing things. There's a …"

Yet before she could continue, Rosso interrupted.

"If I don't eat soon I think I'm going to pass out."

Taking the tray from the cook, he sat at the trestle table, suggesting to Clare that she should do the same. It was a surreal experience, sitting down breaking bread under the freshly-painted gaze of Jesus. Whatever the Master had just said to His disciples had obvious created a great stir. The disciples looked concerned and confused, but the face of the traitor Judas hadn't been finished yet, which made Rosso think to himself, *I wonder whose face I'd use if anyone asked me to paint the face of that traitor?*

"It's brilliant, isn't it?" Clare remarked.

"You're right. I think it's brilliant too," Rosso agreed.

The nuns showed Rosso to his cell, whilst they took Clare to the enclosed part of the convent.

"You'll be safe here, little sister," he said. "I have to arrange for a fresh horse for tomorrow. I don't like the look of the weather, so we'll need to leave at the crack of dawn—before the weather breaks."

Lifting her, he gave her a big hug, and put her down, watching as she headed off down the corridor, in the company of a young nun.

Rosso was headed out the gate when the gatekeeper called him to one side.

"Are you two traveling alone, or are you expecting companions?"

"No. We're on our own, and we'll be leaving soon. Why?"

"I wouldn't be doing my job correctly if I didn't let some people in and keep other people out," he said "But shortly after you arrived, three men came up that street and stood at the other side of the piazza—just as brazen as if they were proper locals. They weren't locals as sure as eggs is eggs, but it's my belief that they were watching this place. And not only that," he added in a lower voice, "I reckon I'd know a Spaniard when I saw one, and those men were Spaniards. Otherwise, I'm a Dutchman."

He pulled up his trousers.

"Look—no wooden clogs, there my boy!" he said, giving the young monk a knowing wink.

"Spaniards?" Rosso mused. "I don't know any Spaniards. Perhaps they were looking for someone else."

The gatekeeper inclined his head to one side and gave Rosso a knowing look.

"So be it, but if I see them again, do you want me to let you know?"

"Yes, why not," Rosso answered, trying to sound as casual as he could, though he felt uneasy.

The idea of strangers following them—whilst he saw no sight on them on the journey, gave him cause for real concern.

"Any idea where I might get a horse around here?" he asked the gatekeeper.

"Why don't you try down at the Duomo Cathedral? It's right in the centre of Milan and not far from here."

After providing directions, he continued.

"It really is one huge building site, but there are lots of tradesmen and merchants of all types down there. I reckon it should be fairly easy to find someone who'd sell you a horse—for the right *price*, that is."

Having thanked the gatekeeper for his kindness and help, Rosso set off for the Duomo. He was not prepared for what he saw. The soaring heights and marbled walls of the Duomo took his breath away. The Cathedral inspired awe from the outside, whilst to walk inside was to enter into the world of the spirit. The whole area was alive with masons, carpenters, bronze-makers, guilders, sculptors, artists and every conceivable craftsman that could create and do justice to such a magnificent monument to their God.

Rosso went through the throng and found what he was looking for—a horse trader with an honest face. That particular horse trader was about ten years old, but going on 30. He had a ragged cap perched on his head, and he was removing the last traces of flesh from the leg bone of a chicken. Tethered next to him, there were two reasonably healthy-looking horses who were munching on their fodder.

"Are either of these horses for sale?" he asked

"Depends who's asking?" came the cheeky reply.

"A poor monk who has to go to the monastery in Como," Rosso replied, thinking again of the many sins he would soon have to repent. *It's very hard trying to live in this world and not tell a lie*, he mused to himself.

The boy scrutinized him.

"Are you sure you're a *proper* monk? You don't look very monkish to me."

He paused, suspicious of the red-headed, travel-worn man in a tattered habit.

"Are you trying to pull one over me?"

"I can assure you that I am *definitely* a monk, and I definitely need a horse. And not only that, I'm on the Duke's business," he insisted with his fingers crossed behind his back. "How much for *that* one?" he said pointing to the stronger looking one of the two.

As they haggled over a price, the lad proved himself to be quite the expert in trading, pleading that he was "only a poor orphan, too, Sir." Yet then, with a wink, he said that he'd have to ask his *father* to check if the price was "okay."

Whilst he was waiting for an answer from the absent father, Rosso saw a group of men sitting at a nearby taverna, one of whom had been watching them closely from under the penumbra of his big felt hat. The boy went over to that man and began an animated discussion—the upshot of which was that the man gave his son a cuff around the ears. The boy returned to answered Rosso with a wry grin.

"He's happy."

"I wouldn't like to see him when he's not happy then," Rosso said.

The boy replied with a tired look in his eyes.

"No mister, you *wouldn't*."

In all the time they spoke, the father never took his eyes off them. The deal was cemented with a handshake, and Rosso handed the money over. Then, on an impulse, Rosso whispered to the boy.

"Look, if I can ever be of any help you to—Brother Rosso's my name. You take care of yourself."

He led the horse away and walked slowly back to the Convent. As he moved away from the main piazza the density of the crowds grew scarcer until the echoing street was filled with the hypnotic sounds of the horse's hooves on cobbled stones.

As he walked past the large double-door entrance of a merchant's storehouse—doors with a small gate—two masked men appeared out of the door. Rosso stood frozen in place spot as they grabbed him by the arm and bundled him through the narrow entrance into the silent court-yard behind. Then something hit him hard on his head and everything went black.

He roused himself to find one of the men going through his clothes and the other whisper, in Spanish, shouting to his co-conspirator.

"Well, did you find it?"

A guttural growl suggested that the searcher hadn't found anything.

"Where have you put it?" the captor asked Rosso Italian, his foul-breathing face just inches away.

"I've no idea what you are talking about," Rosso slurred in reply. "I'm a monk, and I've no idea what you're talking about," he repeated, despite feeling nauseous and becoming aware of the sensation of warm blood running down his neck.

The familiar sound of a blade ringing close to his ear and the touch of cold steel pressed against his throat cleared his mind instantly. It was not fear, but the certainty that, at last, he had nothing more to fear. If he was to die in the next few seconds, then so be it. During his time in the monastery, he learned about the gift of abandonment to Gods will—something that once seemed abstract and unreal. But in the very moment the blade touched his neck, he knew what abandonment really was, and he smiled into his assassin's face.

There was a noise at the gate. The sounds of shouting voices were followed by a violent banging on the door. The would-be assassins looked toward each other and melted into the shadows at the back of the yard just as the door burst open. Rushing through the door was the father of the young horse trader, who looked at the bloodied bundle that was his erstwhile customer, and gave a grunt as if to say, "*I knew you'd come to no good.*"

Glancing around to see if they were still alone, he helped Rosso to sit up and checked his head for the source of the blood.

"Luckily it was your head they hit—it's the farthest point from your brains. It don't look very pretty, but it's not fatal… I think."

He turned to his son.

"You boy, take that horse back home and gets some clean rags, cos this red-headed wonder will need some cleaning up."

He put his arms around Rosso, helping him back along the street. The young lad rode Rosso's horse ahead, as if he was the Duke of Milan, but when he turned to see if they were still following, Rosso thought he saw the hint of fear in the young lad's eyes.

When they reached the dwelling place of the horse trader a few streets away, entering through an abused front door, Rosso slumped down onto a wooden stool near the only window. To him, it felt as if no fresh air had entered that boxed-up space for years. The rancid atmosphere reeked with the sweet but fetid smell of horse manure and hay, which emanated from abandoned clothes that lay piled high in one corner. The flies were the only creatures that seemed to relish the atmosphere in the small confines of the kitchen. The boy reappeared with the clean rags and handed them carefully to his father who sneered.

"Get off with you now and leave im to me!"

"But Dad…" the boy began.

He stopped mid-sentence when he saw the threatening, upraised fist of his father.

"Young boys need a firm hand eh," the man said with a grin that revealed his yellowed teeth. "But tell me, dear Brother, what was it that those villains were after?"

The sudden change in his manner from violent father to unctuous host jarred every nerve in Rosso's still reeling mind.

"They obviously hit on the wrong man," the man said, half-smiling at his own humor.

"I've no idea who they were or what they wanted," Rosso answered, cringing. "But my thanks to you for your help in my hour of need—otherwise, I don't know what would have happened next."

"There're not too many red-headed monks around, so it's hard to imagine that they had the wrong fellow," the father said, his nervous eyes darting questioning looks at Rosso, all the time wringing his hands and feigning friendliness.

"Perhaps they're color-blind," Rosso answered, trying to deflect his less-than-savory savior.

The sound of something falling came from a back room.

"Is that your wife?" Rosso asked.

"I hopes as not. She's been dead this past five years," the man replied. "But I'll go and check. You just sit there and get your wind back."

He left the kitchen, accompanied by half of the resident flies, to investigate the source of the noise. As soon as he'd left the room, Rosso was startled by the sight of a head that appeared behind the murky panes that served as the window of the kitchen. With the light coming straight at him, it took a few seconds to realize that it was the young boy.

"Get out of ere," the boy hissed. "It's a trap. Just get out of ere now!" and the face disappeared.

Confusion filled the monk's battered brain, but he stumbled towards the door just as the noise from the rear became louder and the sound of low voices with foreign accents reached his ears. Exiting the kitchen as quietly as he could, he rounded the corner to see the young lad at the edge of the yard, beckoning for him to hurry for his life.

Rosso made a dash for the exit just as the father appeared at the kitchen door, along with the two villains who attacked him earlier. Reaching the street, Rosso searched for the boy and saw him lurking in a doorway. Running as fast as his legs could carry him, he ducked into the alleyway where his little friend was waiting.

"Quick, follow me," the boy whispered as he set off through the alleyways and laneways of Milan. "They'll never keep up with us here. This is my territory," he said, tapping the side of his nose.

As if by magic, they arrived at the Piazza of the Chiasa Di Santa Maria della Grazia, where they paused to get their breath.

"You was led into a trap," the boy said. "I'd heard mi old man talking with them villains earlier, and they had it all worked out. You was to be caught up, and if they got lucky, then they'd get whatever it was what they was lookin for. But if they couldn't get it— whatever it was—then they was goin to let you go, cos that way, you'd be put you off-guard and spill the beans to the guy who was to get you away. That's where mi ole man comes in. I dunno what you have, but it's gotta be important, cos the old man don't trust nobody, and he was as thick with those three blokes. They must've give him a lot of coin to get him so sweet."

After delivering the insightful message, he turned to left, but Rosso stopped him with a firm grip on his shoulder.

"You saved my life, little man. I owe you a great deal. Thank you."

The tall red-headed monk reached out to his small young rescuer and grasped his hand before they parted as friends. From a little way off, the boy turned and shouted back to Rosso.

"I'll get that orse to you in the morning—the ole man don't deserve to ave it and yer money too!"

As Rosso stumbled across the piazza, his head was really beginning to throb.

This is starting to get serious!

By the time he reached convent gates, he almost fell into the arms of the porter.

"I see that your friends found you," the latter volunteered, grimly sizing-up the wounded wanderer.

"You'd better get in here quick. Mother Superior will want to know about this quick smart."

He bundled Rosso inside the convent and glanced up and down the street to make sure that there were no hired spies watching.

They made their way to the Refractory, where word of Rosso's arrival had already reached the Mother Superior, who soon appeared at Rosso's side. Lifting his head from cupped hands, he was surprised at what he saw. For some reason, he had thought that Mother would be tall and imposing, but he saw a small woman, whose face was unlined, and yet it bore an owlish expression.

"I find that one of the challenges of being a religious is we often find ourselves banging our heads against a brick wall. But you, dear brother, seem to be making it a lifetime vocation," she said with a wry smile as she lifted his soiled bandages to examine the wound. "It's nothing that some clean dressings and a quiet life for a few days won't fix," she continued, and with the gentlest of hands, she washed, cleaned and re-dressed the wound.

"I am deeply in your debt, Mother, but I have to leave tomorrow."

After a pause to allow her to finish her bandaging, he added, "Very early tomorrow."

The little nun had pale grey eyes, which were haloed by a rim of fragile blue skin, suggesting a greater age than he suspected. Yet behind them, Rosso also glimpsed a deep wisdom. She looked steadily at her patient, but she asked no questions.

"Oft times our Lord calls us to carry a heavy cross, but He has always measured the weight of that cross to match our abilities and our faith in Him. I suspect that you're carrying such a weight. It's not for me to question God's reasons, but merely to help His will be done in the short time that I spend on this earth. You have my blessing, Brother, and my heartfelt prayers go with you and your little companion."

After she had given him a blessing, she rose to leave, pausing, as if reflecting, before concluding.

"That little girl has a beautiful heart and will do wonderful things. Take good care of her, Brother. She is your Pearl of great price."

She left, leaving only the soft sound of the habit blessing the floor as a final benediction.

It was getting late, so Rosso sent a message to the gatekeeper to expect a small boy to arrive with a horse in the early hours of the morning. He hoped that the horse could be fed, watered and prepared for departure soon after that. Then he went to his cell, knelt by the bed, and prayed. This was how the gatekeeper found him slumped over the bed in the black time that preceded the dawn.

"Are you awake brother?"

The whispered growl came through the door, accompanied by a determined knock.

"Are you awake, because your horse an jockey have arrived?"

He pushed the cell door open and entered. He carried a lit candle in front of him, which cast light and shadows into the enveloping gloom.

"Jesus Christ help us and save us!" he whispered under his breath. "Are you okay? You look shocking awful."

"I'm fine," Rosso lied.

His head throbbed like a thousand drums had been playing inside it all night. He slowly got to his feet, steadied by the gatekeeper.

"I'd best tell Mother about this. You ain't fit to knock snow off a rope, let alone ride a horse to the edge of the city," he scolded.

"No," Rosso insisted. "Don't tell anyone until after we've left. I'll be fine. I just need a few minutes to wash my face, and I'll be fine."

He was not fine, yet his will was stronger than his flesh, so he walked out of the cell and toward the Refectory where he waited for Clare.

He was surprised to see the little girl seated, apparently in deep conversation with the Mother Superior. Whatever it was that they were discussing, she didn't look up to see who entered the room, keeping her eyes fixed on Mother. Rosso watched the scene before raising his gaze to look at the fresco, high above them on the gable wall. In the flickering shadows of the candle light, the Disciples seemed more animated than usual, but the figure of Christ was still, and to Rosso, it seemed that He was not listening to the men around Him, but rather watching over the small group in front of Him. Amidst all the turmoil that surrounded Him, He seemed to be the epicenter of a peace that reached down and engulfed all three.

"We thought you might have needed a lie in, Brother, so we didn't disturb you too early. Clare and I have been sharing our stories, and I think we've both learned a great deal from each other. Should you come back this way, then I'd be delighted to hear more from our little friend, and I think we could perhaps share some things with her too."

The little nun put something in Clare's hand and they embraced, like mother and child.

"Go in peace, child," she said, "and do try and keep this man out of harm's way."

Approaching, she gave her hand and her blessing to Rosso, who received it with a bowed head and a grateful heart.

Their horse was waiting for them at the front gate, and though Rosso looked around for the young boy, there was no sight of him. Rosso was certain, however, that the boy was watching from some shadowy laneway as he whispered a prayer for his safety. Clare climbed up on the horse in front of Rosso before the animal trotted off. With every foot-fall of the horse's hooves, the sounds hit Rosso's brain like hammer. He waved thanks and farewell to the convent before they headed out into the rising dawn of the city of Milan, headed south towards the countryside and the coast.

They hadn't been riding for long before Rosso slipped into a waking nightmare. The sight of the sun seemed to pierce his eyes with a searing terror, the desire for sleep was becoming overwhelming and the road ahead seemed to twist and turn before his eyes.

"If I fall asleep, do whatever you need to do to wake me up," he said to Clare, or at least he thought he'd said it, so he said it again to be certain.

The young girl turned around, but instead of seeing her face, he saw the face of the Mother Superior. Confused, he blinked and rubbed his eyes until Clare reappeared, but her face seemed calm.

"I'm going to hop down and lead the horse so you can rest in the saddle."

Rosso was too tired to argue, so the little girl led the half-conscious monk for the rest of the morning until she found somewhere safe they could sleep for the night.

Clare's life had been terrible until that fateful day that her stepfather left her in the piazza in Rome, but life had taught her how to survive. She understood how to find hide-away places that most people would never notice, where she could stay unknown and unharmed for hours at a time. The situation with Rosso was more of a challenge, as she also had a horse and a delirious monk to worry about, but she was a resourceful child, and she had her instructions.

The conversation she had with Mother earlier was to prepare Clare for such an eventuality. Mother had told her in her calm, certain way that if Rosso survived the next 48 hours, then everything would be fine. If he didn't survive, Clare should return to the convent to spend some time with Mother, who would help discern her future.

Clare led the horse away from the road and up into the hills until she found what she was looking for—a small cavern, hidden from the spying eyes of passing travelers, thieves or villainous Spaniards. She helped break Rosso's fall from the horse and guided him into the dry cave, where she found a safe place to lay him down. Leading the horse to a secluded, well-grassed, nearby spot, she tethered it to a stout bush. Taking the blanket from the saddle and some water and victuals from the bags, she went back into the cave to make her companion as comfortable as she possibly could.

Rosso was groaning to himself and seemed to be slipping into the grip of a fever, so Clare lay him down, moped his brow with water and made him suck on a cloth, dipped in the water. She hummed scraps of songs she'd heard the women sing to their babies when they were sick or teething, trying to soothe the pained and bruised brain of poor Rosso.

She tried to imagine what Laura or Mother at the convent would have done, holding his hand until he fell asleep. When she was sure that he was unconscious, she released his hand and crept out to check that the horse was still secure and out of sight. She had chosen the spot well. He was behind the hill, in a small copse, where the leaf mould dampened the sound of his hooves, and the dappled light added to the sense of camouflage.

Moving into the shade of the hill, she watched the road for signs of any movement. The road from Milan to Genoa was an important one for goods traveling to and from that busy port. She watched as carts, laden with silks and spices, rumbled past from the south, whilst others, heavily-laden with wheat and wood, rattled back towards the port, from the north. There was a drowsy sort of symmetry to this slow, yet steady coming and going that brought Clare to the verge of dozing off, when suddenly the horsemen came galloping along the road.

She counted three of them, although Rosso had only spoken of there being two, but there was something about them and their sense of urgency that made her shrink further into the shadows. When they were almost level with her, the front horseman slowed and studied the fields on either side. When he looked directly at the spot where she was hiding, she felt very small and vulnerable, holding her breath, but the moment passed. His two companions caught up, the three headed down the road at a fast trot.

That was scary! she thought, as she dropped the stone that she had in her hand before heading back to check on her patient. Being a resourceful girl, she knew how to light a fire that wouldn't give off any smoke, and she'd lit the fire inside the cave to provide heat for Rosso and to warm her own thin frame. She was surprised how cool the cave was only a few feet from the entrance, and by how dry it was. Holding up a flaming stick from the flickering fire, she crept slowly around the cave, discovering signs of previous occupants who had sought shelter in the past. To her great relief, she found no traces of wolves or bears. Walking back to the entrance to the cave, she sat down to watch the evening draw on, and slowly she drifted off to sleep.

She woke as the sun was going down, angry with herself for being so weak. When she checked on Rosso, he was resting peacefully. *He'll heal whilst he sleeps*, she thought to herself as she prepared a small meal.

When Rosso eventually awoke, he thought he was still in his cell in Milan, but when he tried to sit up his bruised body and the duck egg-sized lump on his head recalled him to the present. As his eyes grew accustomed to the light of the fire, he saw his little mother, near the entrance, staring out into space.

"I could eat a horse and chase the rider," he said. "I'm so hungry! How long have I been out cold?"

"All *day!*" she answered with a big grin on her face. "And you snore," she said whilst rising to bring him fresh water and food. "I'm surprised those men didn't hear you and come up to see what all the noise was about."

"I hope it wasn't those two who attacked me," he replied. "I don't think my skull could take another battering like that."

"There were *three*—not two," she said.

"Three?" he exclaimed. "Then the boy who sold me the horse wasn't wrong when he said three."

He paused, muttering to himself.

"And three onto one isn't good odds, especially as that one is now about a half."

"But you've got me, too," piped up his little companion, who could hear a pin drop at fifty paces. "And I know how to defend myself," she added.

Rosso looked at her, trying to imagine what it would have been like for a little girl to have survived what she suffered through. *The two of us have so much in common*, he thought, and that made him more determined to make sure that no more harm would come to her.

"They might have the numbers, but we've got the brains eh?" he said, grinning in a way that beckoned reciprocation.

"Why do you think they are following you, Rosso" she asked

He had been expecting the question, but he still didn't have a clear idea of how he would answer. Gazing at her face in the orange glow of the fire, he saw a little child. He had seen her play like a little child too. Yet he also saw in the face of that angelic little child—the child who sat so quietly while listening to the Mother—a face suggested to him that she could handle the truth.

"I've been asked by someone very important to go on a secret mission to another very important person, and I think those men out there are trying to stop me," he confessed, pointing in the direction of the highway.

"Oh, you mean you're taking a message from the Pope to the King of France," she said matter-of-factly.

"How on Earth?..."

His words dried up as his mouth dropped open.

"Well," she said as if she was explaining something very complicated to a little child. "Mother and I had a little chat this morning, and afterwards, she said that was what you were probably doing. She also said that I should help you as much as I could, because you were almost certainly going to get into a lot of trouble by the way you were going about everything."

As she spoke, she shook her finger at him, as if to admonish him for getting his skull cracked open.

When the implications of this little conspiracy against him sank in, he smiled, and that smile turned into a chuckle, and that chuckle grew into a soul-relieving, head-clearing, life-affirming laugh.

"You cannot believe what a relief it is to not to have to deceive you," he said as he struggled to his feet, walked around the camp fire and gave her a hug. "Women," he added, "Monks can't live with them, but we can't survive without them," at which they both laughed.

"We need to make plans for the morning," he said. "It should only take a couple of days to reach Genoa now that I'm starting to feel strong again, but we need to work out how to avoid those men who are chasing us."

"Mother said you would be great in the circus," Clare said with a sideways, knowing grin.

"Huh?" he replied, sensing there was more to what she had said than the implied descriptive slight.

"Mother said you would be great in the circus—the circus that's been traveling around Lombardy... *and is going back to France in the next couple of days*. She said they'd surely snap up an entertainer like you any day," she added, dissolving into childish giggles, whilst Rosso blushed at the comment.

"I'm glad I've taken my vows, Otherwise, I might use some very un-Christian language right now!" he countered, attempting to sound earnest, but failing badly. "But it sounds like a fantastic idea, though."

Raising his eyes towards heaven he concluded.

"It's at times like this that I strongly suspect that God might be a woman, after all."

They woke the next morning to the sound of larks, calling out from the clear blue skies. They broke their fast and broke their camp before heading back to the road. The day was fresh and clear, so they made good time, with only a few stops for food and to rest their aching limbs. As they went along Rosso shared more stories of his youth, reading in Clare's expressions of empathy.

Clare turned her wise face towards him as they rode along.

"It's funny, isn't it? If I hadn't lived that life when I was little, then I would never have met you, or Sara and Marco, or Mother either. But now I couldn't imagine my world without any of you, which is really strange, isn't it?"

Moving in unison with the rhythmic rocking of the horse, Rosso eyed his little companion.

"And I couldn't imagine a world without you either, little lady."

When they neared Genoa, it wasn't difficult to discover where the circus was. Elephants and lions are difficult beasts to hide, even in a city. When they arrived, the big top was in the process of being taken down, and the well-rehearsed ritual of the crew packing it up and putting it away had been going on for the previous two days.

The circus people looked ordinary as they went about their work, a far cry from the painted people who flew from post to post high above the crowds, or the tumblers who jumped through lighted hoops each night. But one such figure was the same—in his makeup *and* without it. Rosso's heart lit up with joy when he saw him.

"Odysseo!" he cried out to the little man.

There remained some traces of make up on the dwarf's face that made it look t sadder than normal. But when he heard his name being called and saw who was calling him, a smile dissipated the sadness, and his face lit up with delight.

"Well, look what the donkey dropped," he said and walked towards them with his waddling gait. "Who's your young friend?" he said, quietly pleased to have someone who he could look straight in the eye.

"Clare, this is Odysseo," said Rosso. "And Odysseo, this is my brave companion, Clare. We're on our way to Paris to see if we can find her father or mother."

Bowing towards Clare, he welcomed her to his circus and inquired as to how long he might have the pleasure of her company. Clare giggled at his words, but then saw the elephant, her eyes opened wide, like saucers.

"It's *huge!*" she whispered, taking a step back to stand beside Rosso.

"Allow me to introduce you," the dwarf said impishly.

He leaned casually against the elephant's stumpy leg and fed it a banana that he magically produced from under his hat.

"Hannibal, meet Clare—one of Rome's finest!"

He laughed.

"But I don't think it's fair that the elephant gets all the food while my two guests stand there with empty stomachs. Come on! Let's go and find something to eat."

Taking Clare by the hand, the odd couple waddled off in front of Rosso to the camp kitchen.

With Clare happily ensconced with the motherly figure of the lion tamer's wife, Odysseo signaled with his eyes to Rosso that perhaps they might step outside and have a quiet discussion.

"Before you say anything, be careful, because there are eyes and ears everywhere, and not all of them are of a friendly disposition," he said quietly.

He settled his squat figure on a bale of straw and invited Rosso to take an upturned bucket opposite him. They were out in the open, away from any malign eavesdroppers, and they could observe everyone as they came and went.

"For a monk and a knife-sharpener, you're a lousy liar," he said to Rosso, who reddened at the remark.

"I'm on my way to Paris to meet with someone very important there. But apparently someone, or some people don't want the meeting to take place. I don't know why— perhaps they just don't like the way I dress," he said, trying to lighten the mood." But since we started out, I've been attacked once, and as far as I can gather, we've been followed all the way from Rome."

Picking up an apple he bit a chunk before continuing.

"It looks like there are three riders, but only two of them attacked me. I don't know what happened to the third. Anyway, I escaped with the help of some unexpected friends, and whilst I was raving in a cave with the child looking after me, they went on ahead, searching for us. My suspicion is that they're Spanish. That's why we need to get on the next boat to Marseilles."

"I'm glad to hear that not much has changed and that you're still raving," Odysseo said with overt glee, punching his hat into an unrecognizable shape. "Perhaps it's your red hair that attracts trouble, you know—like moths. But unfortunately in this case, the moths ride horses and carry nasty, sharp swords!"

Odysseo stared at the mis-shapen mass that had once been his hat, becoming more serious.

"Getting you on the boat will be no problem, because once we get you out of those clothes and put a wig on that carrot top of yours, then everyone will know you're just another circus clown."

Fisting his hat once more, marveling at his own brilliance, he rocked around on the hay bale in mock laughter.

"When do you leave?" Rosso asked, smiling at his friends humor, though trying to look hurt at the same time. "Because it's not just about me getting to Paris. This child really is looking for her parents, and all we have to go on is that her father's a French noble, and that she has a remarkable birthmark, which we're hoping either her mother or father also has."

"Now I know why monks believe in miracles," the dwarf replied. "But for once, I believe you. We sail in the morning, depending on the weather. Most of the equipment will be on the boat by this evening, which is also probably the best time for you to slip you on board. That way, you can be on the lookout for those Spaniards when the rest of the passengers embark tomorrow."

Having laid their plans, Odysseo led Rosso back to the camp. There, they found everything packed and ready to go. If anyone had been watching when they left for the dockside, they might have noticed that the group's number had increased by two—a tall clown with a sad face, an orange wig and a battered hat, and a little girl, leading an elephant whilst feeding it apples.

The dockside was loud and smelt of rope, spices, tar and sweat. It was dangerous though exciting. There were people who bore loads on their backs and others who pushed loads on their barrows, whilst there were also people who would cut your throat as fast as they could cut your purse. So whilst Rosso and Clare soaked up all the hustle and bustle, the scents and the sights, they kept a close eye on each other and on lookout for their pursuers.

Finding the boat that was to take them to Marseilles, they helped carry the remaining baggage up its short, steep, wooden boarding plank. All aboard were busy preparing the vessel for departure, with crewmen hurrying late stores below decks, and all around, there were loud shouts and fierce looks.

By evening time, Rosso, Clare and Odysseo had squared their possessions away and had retired to the safety of their hammocks. Only one small candle lit the passenger deck as they fell asleep, listening to the slap of ropes against the mast in the cool night breezes.

In addition to the circus people, there were other passengers traveling to Marseilles, and these came on board the following morning. There was an old woman with a crumpled face and hollowed cheeks, whose moist, ghost cough caused her to frequently smother her face and reach for the old rag she carried in her pocket. Her companion had that redness of cheek that crept up around his glassy eyes, which suggested an intimate association with an excess of alcoholic beverages the previous night. He was fidgety, thirsty, and edgy, and his fingers tugged at his neckerchief, as if it were several sizes too small.

Clare eyed a young lad nearby, who like all lads of his generation, had an intriguing interest in the contents of his nose. He wore cut-off canvas trousers, held up by a thin leather belt that had been cut down to size to suit his lean frame. He also wore a cambric shirt several sizes too big for him, and he went barefoot, as was required of all reputable seamen! He had sharp features—a head of jet black hair, that defied any attempts at domestication, and a quick eye that finally settled on Clare and her companion.

"Are you with the circus mob," he said, jerking one of his non exploratory fingers towards the hold where the circus crew had their quarters.

Clare wandered over to him.

"Is this your ship?"

Each waited for the other to answer first.

"Does it go very fast?" Clare continued, ignoring the boy's attempt at an imposing posture.

Her question found its mark in his sailor's pride, so tucking his hands into his pocket, he answered.

"She's not pretty, but when the wind gets behind them sails, she fair sweeps over the waves."

"Does she have a name?" Clare inquired.

"She's the Santa Maria, and I'm the captain's main man" he said with pride.

"And does the captain's main man have a name?" she asked.

"Kristopher's mi real name, but seeing as how the ship's cat is also called Kristopher, the crew calls me Puss—which ain't a particular nice name, but then they don't know what I calls them behind their backs neither!"

As he spoke, Clare could see the face of the young boy that he really was.

"Will you show me around your ship, please, Kristopher?" she asked.

He replied with a wide and happy grin.

"Be delighted too, young lady. But don't worry bout calling me Puss—I kinda got used to it over the past couple of years. Wot's your name, then, seeing as how we's now on first name terms?"

"Everyone calls me Clare," she said, and then, taking him by the hand, she continued, "Well, come on then."

"T'will do him the world of good having a young mate for a while," a voice called over Rosso's shoulder. He turned and found the ship's mate, whose eyes were following the youngsters as they disappeared down into one of the front holds.

"T'ain't right for a young lad to spend so much time with rough folk like we sailors at his age."

He looked into Rosso face.

"Marseilles is it, then?"

As he was uncertain as to whether it was a question or a statement, Rosso nodded.

"Been on a ship before?"

That was definitely a question, so Rosso replied.

"Where I grew up, *everyone* had webbed feet."

The statement drew a wry grin from the gnarled sailor.

"You must be a Venetian then," he said with a degree of admiration. "So rough water shouldn't be of any concern to the likes of you two. She your sister or what?" he asked with a hint of suspicion in his voice.

"She's my sister," said Rosso but didn't embellish this statement with any further facts.

An Irishman who studied with him at the monastery always said *a shut mouth catches no flies*, and Rosso lived by that saying, believing it wise to say little and listen much.

Realizing he wasn't going to get any more information from the quiet clown, the mate went off to check out on his other passengers, but he paused halfway, shouting back.

"You'd better go and check on your hammocks below. You don't want any of this mob pinching em whilst your back's turned. It's not often we have our friends from Venice on board."

He gave Rosso a wink and, pleased with his own sense of humour, proceeded to carry on with his nautical duties.

When the two child explorers returned, they went with Rosso below, with Puss scooting amongst all the tackle, leading them to the "Best ammicks on this ere ship!—better than them what you ad last night. These uns is further from the slop buckets, and they stink a'rter a couple of ours."

Above, there was a sudden commotion on the deck, accompanied by much shouting and then the clanking sound of a chain being lifted.

"The wind must'a changed. That's the lads pulling up the anka!" Puss explained before dashing up the stairs and disappearing onto the deck.. Rosso followed Clare, attempting to keep up, and in the process he lost the first of many pieces of skin from the top of his cranium as it hit the lower beams of the ship's skeleton.

On deck, there was chaos, with those who knew what to do shouting crude invectives at those who didn't know what to do.

"Clear the decks! Else you'll get thrown overboard afore we leave port!"

It signaled for the passengers to congregate like sheep at the aft of the ship, waiting until it was safer to move about the boat.

There was something wonderful about a boat getting under sail—the crack of the canvas as the wind snapped it into shape, the sawing sound of sisal ropes as they ran through the wooden pulleys, and the lurch of the hulking beast as the power of nature transformed the ugly dockside monster into a thing of serene beauty as in majesty, she breathed in the wind and powered over the water. Only then came the realization that the boat had a voice. It creaked and squeaked in a gentle swell, but groaned and moaned when the menacing waves were dazzling white with foam.

Rosso and Clare stood with the rest of the motley travelers, relieved that there was not a Spaniard amongst them, soaking up the experience. In time, the port receded from their sight, whilst overhead the swirl of wailing gulls grew less and less in number, and slowly the land disappeared from sight.

Life on board a small boat left no room for privacy, a concept unknown to small children, who were oblivious to the polite practice of personal intimacies. For Rosso, however, his time in the monastery had prepared him well for the trip. Hustled below deck with strangers, shut off from the light of day, the constant movement of the boat and the unexpected smells combined to create an atmosphere that was at once claustrophobic, and yet cozy

The hierarchy of the small band of fellow travelers was soon established, but the mighty colossus that was Odysseo's personality remained curiously withdrawn. He informed Rosso, on one of the few occasions that he showed his face, that for those such as he, invisibility was the better option when there was no safe exit to be found. He added, with his terrible smile, "And we dwarves are not renowned swimmers!"

Amongst the other passengers, there were those who wished to share all they had, and they did so happily. Others were happy in their own isolation, and there were a few whose very presence seemed to inoculate that disparate band of exiles with their own doubts, fears and antipathies.

A routine was established. Dawn meant an early start—the passengers had a meal, and then they cleared the decks below of refuse and the nightly accumulations of bodily excretions. As far as was possible, they let fresh air into that enclosed space, bringing the bedding up, to be aired in the sunshine and sea breeze. And finally, each person found time to conclude what they wished to conclude.

For Rosso, it was his daily prayers and readings, and he supplemented the routine by writing in a journal he started when he met Clare. A secret part of him wished to share everything he did with his dearest sister, Agnes, but his justification was because he thought Clare would need some record of her early life, to give her a sense of belonging.

Clare spent her spare time with Puss, who delighted in showing her the "scariest" part of the ship, which they found at the top of the highest mast. But life in the crow's nest showed her a world that thrilled her with vast horizons and clear blue skies. She told Rosso that she had never felt so free in all her short life as when she did up in the "nest." She was always reluctant to climb back down onto the deck when it was time for lunch.

"Up there, I feel I can almost touch the sky, and that makes me feel so big and brave. And when I look down—all the grown-ups who growl and grumble at me just for having some fun—they all look like little ants down on the deck."

In the afternoon, passengers returned the bedding below the deck as the cooks prepared a small evening meal. Some talked, while others dozed, strolled about the small deck or played games of dice or cards. The repeated routine had a slowing effect for all on board. With little else to worry about, time seemed to pass easier with the sun following its benign course across the sky and the moon returning the compliment at night.

When they sighted land, they did so with a mixture of excitement and regret. No storms from the heavens had disturbed them, and even the threatened squalls, caused by human selfishness, failed to surface or to ruffle the peace that had been the hallmark of the crossing. Marseilles grew in size as the gulls swooped down on the city, crying their welcome from that ancient human melting pot, founded so long ago by the venerable Greeks of mystery.

As the ship's captain maneuvered his small vessel into one of the vacant berths, coils of rope snaked out to snare it to the land. Planks appeared and the passageway cleared for passengers to disembark. Rosso sought out Odysseo and found him perched on a coil of ropes, watching the animals being unloaded. He thanked his friend for helping them on their way.

"You never mentioned Villeprieux," the dwarf whispered into Rosso's ear as he stooped to give him a farewell hug. "Men like him can be difficult to kill. I'm not saying he's still alive—just that he's been in tight places before, and yet he always managed to come out with full pockets and unblemished skin."

His face changed, as if a dark mood had lifted.

"I'll say no more on that subject, but if I'm any judge of men, then I'd have to say you were born under a lucky star—your current hairstyle excepted. As for that gem of a girl with you—treasure her, Rosso. Treasure her."

Clearing his throat, he stared past his friend, roaring to the handlers.

"Be careful with my elephant, you ignorant brute!"

Giving Rosso a wink, he cocked his head.

"Business calls!"

Slipping from his perch, he scooted off down the gang-plank, shouting orders as he went.

When Clare appeared on deck, she seemed sad.

"Has Odysseo gone? I'll really miss him."

She waved at his disappearing figure, who suddenly stopped when she'd mentioned his name. Taking off his hat, he punched it, waved it back at her, turned and was lost in the throng on the quay. Clare looked up at Rosso.

"There's something I've got to do! Wait here!"

She took off, weaving amongst the mob on the crowded deck, and found her quarry, leaning against the port side rail, with his thumbs hitched under his thin leather belt, the eastern breeze tugging at his spiky salted hair.

From a distance, Rosso watched her lean towards him and say something into his ear. It was only a few words, but it gave birth to a wide grin on the boy's face. He turned to her and said a few words before she spun on her feet, headed back towards Rosso.

"What did you say to him?" he asked.

"Nothing," she replied.

"Well, what did he say to you then?" Rosso asked, attempting to unravel the mystery.

"Nothing," she said, and taking hold of his hand, they went down the bucking plank, plunging into the chaos.

Down on the dockside, they joined the discordant dance of those who knew where they were going along with those who did not. Suppliers were hawking their wares, sailors were either going up or coming down something, and families were either saying "goodbye" with tears or "hello" with even more tears—but there was one man who was doing none of those things.

He seemed to be idling on a barrel, sharpening a stick with a knife, whilst now and again making furtive glances towards the very ship that Rosso and Clare had disembarked. Rosso thought he was a cutpurse, looking for a vulnerable victim, so he held Clare's hand firmly. She was oblivious to any lurking dangers in dockyards and dark places.

Yet Rosso forgot all thoughts of this feral creature in the hurly burly of throngs on the docks. He needed to secure directions to the Abbey where they would stay the night. That was why he didn't see that surly fellow remove his elbow from the barrel and shadow the two as they went on their way.

Farther away from the docks, the crowds dissipated, though the noise of humanity was replaced by the clattering carts on rutted tracks, going into the city to drop off or pick up merchandise. One hem stopped and offered to carry the mendicant monk and his little companion, refusing any suggestion of payment.

"It's human nature, ain't it, to give someone a hand when you can. And seeing as I've got a empty cart, *I* can, if you follow me."

Shrugging his shoulders, the man urged his lazy horse to move on. The cart made their way into the town as the last clouds cleared from the sky, leaving it bright and fresh in the morning air.

Their carrier dropped them near the Abbey and gave them directions about how best reach their destination.

Rosso thanked him for his help, and the carrier replied with ingrained honesty.

"If it's no bother for this old horse of mine, then it ain't no bother to me neither."

"He's a nice man, isn't he?" Clare remarked.

"He surely is!"

Rosso had watched Clare thrive on the journey from Rome, nourished by the experiences and the people they had met along the way. In his few quiet moments, he thought about how far he, to, had come since he was a child like her—of how he'd been blessed to have great teachers, such as Gino, dearest Agnes, Julian, Bart, Fr Alphonsus, and of course, Villeprieux, who'd taught him to speak French in the time they'd been together.

Yet it astonished him how quickly Clare absorbed things and facts. She had picked up a few French words on the trip across, and she was mimicking the French manner-isms as they left the Abbey to find a boat that would take them to Lyon.

"You amaze me, little sister," he said. "If I didn't know any better, I'd say you had French blood in you."

He tousled her hair, eliciting a big grin.

"And if I didn't know, big brother, I'd say that you didn't have a drop of sincerity in your voice at all."

She raced ahead, giggling as he chased after her. Whilst in pursuit, Rosso bumped into a cape-covered man and made to beg pardon for the incident, but he instantly became rooted to the spot: there, standing in front of him, with slightly bored features and handsome face—presently a little ravaged by hard times—stood Francois Villeprieux, Rosso's dearest of friends.

"You're alive!" Rosso whispered, half in joy and half in amazement. "It really *is* you, Villeprieux, isn't it?"

"Well if it isn't, *Maman* will be extremely upset," he replied in an offhand manner. "Actually, *mon cher ami*, I am on my way to see her now. What' is your excuse for being in this rat-infested place?"

Smiling, the dear friends embraced, laughed, and embraced again. It was only when Rosso felt a tug at his habit that they disentangled.

"Who's that?"

Rosso made the formal introductions.

"This, my sweetest of little sisters, is my dearest friend from a long time ago. Allow me to introduce Monsieur Francois Villeprieux—friend, soldier, and my savior."

Clare took a long look at Villeprieux, drew herself up to her full height, and spoke in perfect French.

"*Enchant*é, Monsieur."

"*Moi aussi*," replied the courteous Frenchman, while making a sweeping low bow to the young girl.

"She is your child?" Villeprieux asked with a barely suppressed smirk about his lips.

"No, she's not," laughed Rosso in return. "It's a long story, but the short version is that we're off to Paris to see if we can find her parents."

He put his arm around her, pulling her close.

"And what is this with the black cloak and the shaved spot on top of your head?" Villeprieux patted the bald spot on Rosso's head as a master would pat his dog. You look like a runaway from a traveling circus, or something that farmers put in the fields to scare off the crows!"

Slapping Rosso on the back, he linked his arm and they headed off towards the river port.

"I'm going to Paris too," Villeprieux announced. "It's a long time since I ave seen *ma mere*, and it makes her happy to see me every now and then."

But in his voice, there was no sense of excitement of homecoming. It was more accurate to say that this bored, restless man lacked anything else to interest him at that particular time, and visiting his mother would fill an unwelcome void.

"Do you have a papa too?" Clare asked from the safety of Rosso's other side.

"*Non, ma petite.* He died when I was so very young. I have no memory of him. Perhaps he was a fairy that lives in the woods, and that' is why I find it so difficult to stay in one place."

A moment of honest sadness illuminated his features.

"*Mais, c'est la vie*, and we must do our best, eh Monsieur Monk? Now tell me—how did you come to be dressed up like a real monk? Are you hiding from something or someone?"

"That's a very good question and one that I'm still trying to work out. But yes, it's for real. I'm a novice monk now who's managed to avoid his final vows. To be quite honest, I'm still not one hundred percent certain that I want to commit myself for life to total obedience to an Abbot whom I find it difficult to respect. But that's another story.

"Clare and I are on our way to Paris, but it appears that we're also being chased by some Spanish spies, for reasons that I can't really explain, because it's a still a bit of a mystery to me too. But less about me. What about you? What have you been up to since the battle?"

He paused to remember all the horrors of that awful day.

"I thought you were *dead*—but then I thought the Dom was dead too—and he almost was, until we found him in a terrible state on the streets of Rome."

"The *Dom* is still alive?" Villeprieux interjected with seeming great surprise. "*Sacrebleu!* That is indeed a miracle!"

"Yes," Rosso sighed. "Don't look so guilty. I'm sure there was nothing you could've done to help him. But poor Dom! He was terribly wounded in the battle itself, but then they took him prisoner and tortured him, too. They cut off his sword arm and put out one of his eyes. But it's the emotional scars he carries that are the worst. Thankfully, he's doing well and living with a family who love and care for him."

Rosso paused to reflect.

"Those sorts of things should never happen to someone as peaceable and good as the Dom."

"Why are you crying?" Clare asked, looking up at Rosso.

"It's not tears, little sister. It's just the wind in my eyes."

He squeezed her hand to reassure her.

"But come on, Villeprieux, tell me what you've done and where you've been since that time? By the looks of you, it's pretty obvious that you haven't been living on anyone's doorsteps or entering any monasteries."

"Me a monk? I think not, my friend. I'd be more at home where there are hot fires that never go out" he replied with a cruel laugh that jarred Rosso's nerves. "But no, I don't have to live on anyone's doorstep. I was lucky to escape. I found some friends who helped me a little and gave me some shelter. I travelled here and there, but I got bored with this land of olive oil and fish, so now I go home for a refresh and to speak in my own language. It'll do me good. *C'est tout*—that is all."

Their destination was the last port of call of the mighty River Rhone, on its way from inland France to the Mediterranean Sea. With the river flowed so many stories from centuries past. Popes had passed that way as they dithered between whether to call Avignon or Rome the Eternal City, and home to their mother church. The now abandoned papal palace at Avignon was an empty shell, but the Rhone still flowed past, as if washing away the memories of such human fancies.

They found a boat and set off toward Lyon and from there, the north. The vessel was an old barge with a square rigged sail—the type that was used to transport grain from the countryside to the great cities along its reach. But grain, boats and rivers has one thing in common—rats. The companions had only been on board for a few hours before Clare screamed that she had seen a huge, black rat, the size of a cat.

"But you have us to protect you little one," Villeprieux said as he searched for and skewered the offending rodent.

But rats, like humans, traveled in groups, and the grain ship offered plenty of places for hundreds of them. The journey upstream to Lyon would take some days, which meant that passengers would sleep on the boat, but they'd stop at small ports, wayside stops, to find their food and provisions.

The sleeping quarters were below decks, but Clare was unwilling to settle in those dark dank surroundings with the constant scurrying of tiny feet throughout the night. She and Rosso secured a dry spot on the deck, where they could stretch out and watch the stars pass overhead, leaving VIlleprieux with the other travelers below.

Rosso told her the story of his little Anna and how she had placed a star in the sky for him.

"She was so lucky to have such a kind brother," and moving close to him for warmth, she fell asleep.

After two nights, Villeprieux decided to move his sleeping quarters from below.

"There is such a stench of rats piss, that it's only fit for an Englishman to sleep there," he said, flinging his damp clothes on the dry deck.

Rosso noticed the cuts on his friend's legs and asked what had caused them.

"It is nothing, my friend. A few cuts from the stirrups perhaps, but it will heal quickly once I get the stench of this god-forsaken boat off me."

Two days later, they reached Lyon.

"This is just like Rome," said Clare to Rosso, pointing to the Roman ruins around the town as they sailed into the busy city. "But it's much cleaner. There's more air here."

✛ ✛ ✛

Parting company with the river at Lyon, they searched for the fastest way to travel to Paris. Familiar with the city, Villeprieux told them that he had good friends who would help them get to Paris. Yet all was not well with the Frenchman: he felt sick and began to vomit; a rash appeared on his body and his face was flushed with fever.

Fear stalked their minds. The plague had long used the river to spread its fingers of death into every city, town, and hamlet along its course.

"But I have no lumps, and I'm not black" said the Frenchman. "Look, I'm *red* all over! This is not the plague, but some other trifle."

Beads of perspiration formed on his brow while his eyes held a glazed expression.

"You should stay here until you feel better," Rosso suggested. "Let me go and talk to your friends, and I'll make the arrangements."

For the first time Rosso could remember, Villeprieux seemed uncertain, as if the fever had affected his powers of reason as well.

"No," he said suddenly. "That will not be possible. Only I can go!"

Struggling to his feet, he put on his cloak and set off into the city.

"I don't think we should let him go like that," Clare told Rosso. "Perhaps if we follow him at a distance? Just to make sure he's okay? What do you think, big brother?"

"He won't like it if he finds out," he replied, smiling, and continued, "but who says he'll find out?. Come on, little sister."

Hand in hand, they walked down the shadowy side of the street, pausing when Villeprieux slowed and speeding up when he sped up. Twice Villeprieux stopped and vomitted in the street. Passersby watched, making a wide birth around him.

Those who thought he was drunk gave him foul looks, but no-one approached him. For the first time, Rosso considered his friend frail and vulnerable, feeling pity for him. In all the years he knew Villeprieux, he loved him, admired him, and perhaps in the early days, worshiped him. So he found it strange that the person he exulted was as weak and human as he himself.

Finally, the Frenchman stopped at a staging post. Steadying himself, he went inside. After he had been gone for some time, the unlikely spies took turns exploring the street. It fell to Clare to be the one watching as Villeprieux appeared in the company of two men who wore wide brimmed hats that cast a deep shadow over their faces. The three were in deep conversation but then Villeprieux seemed to disagree, and turning his back, he left. As he did so, one of his companions threw his arms up in disgust—and Clare recognized him at once. She froze for a second before running off to find Rosso.

"We need to head back now. He's just come out, and there's something I must tell you," she said as they hurried down the street together.

"What was it you wanted to tell me?" asked Rosso, but before she could answer, Villeprieux appeared.

"I'll tell you later," she said, and she remained silent until they reached the dock.

If Villeprieux was surprised to see them, he did not show it in his face.

"I ave secured seats on the carriage to Paris, and from there, we will go to my mother's house, not too far away in St Germain en Leys. She will like you because you are *mes amis*, and it will be good for her to see me too."

Being tossed around in a carriage, even a well-sprung one, will test the stamina of the best of souls. But Villeprieux was not well. During the first day of travel, he appeared to improve. The red rash disappeared and his fever abated.

At Rosso's side, Clare listened to the former companions re-tell stories about when they were on the road together, but neither mentioned that final battle. As the journey went on, it began to develop a monotonous routine: they changed horses at various relay stations, they descended from the carriage, stretched, took some food and got back in the carriage. During that time, Rosso never left his sick friend's side. There was no time for Clare to tell him what she had seen and why she had become quiet and withdrawn.

"I hope you've not caught what dear Villeprieux has, little sister," said Rosso during a brief lull, when Villeprieux appeared to have nodded off.

"No, I'm quite well," she replied in a hushed voice, glancing quickly at the sleeping Frenchman. "It's just something

I saw back there in Lyon, and I've been trying to tell you ever since we left…"

"And what *was* it, exactly, that you were trying to tell my little red-headed monk, *ma petite* Clare?" Villeprieux asked from under the shade of the cowl of his hooded cloak.

"Nothing!" Clare snapped, withdrawing into the corner behind the black body of Rosso.

"It's my opinion that little children see and hear far more than we grown-ups realize, but thankfully, they comprehend much less."

With these words VIilleprieux appeared to return to sleep, but Clare said no more for the rest of the journey.

16

CHATEAU VILLEPRIEUX

ARRIVING IN PARIS was like arriving in bedlam— unless you were one of the inmates, and then it was a delight. There were myriad narrow streets, with houses butting against each other across squalid, cobbled bye-ways. There were small stalls and larger markets in every part of that metropolis, where sheep, silks, cheese and cognac were sold to those who could afford them. These privileged peoples, accompanied by maids and man-servants, picked their way through the crowds in their heavily powdered wigs and bonnets, seeming blind to the poverty they passed.

But Villeprieux saw none of it. His sickness had worsed and the whites of his eyes had taken on a faint tinge of yellow. He refused to eat and tired so very easily.

"Let me arrange transport to St Germain, Villeprieux, you're not well enough to do it yourself. Just tell me where to go and I will do it all," Rosso insisted.

His friend tried to stir from the couch at the inn where they had stopped, but he slumped back.

"This is incredible," he said. "When I am white, I'm as strong as an ox, and yet now that I'm yellow, *bien sur*, I'm as weak as a kitten. But do as you will. It seems I must rest and get my strength back before I meet *ma mere*."

He relented, giving Rosso instructions about where he could hire transport to take them to his mother's home.

Clare went with him, and as soon as they left the inn she began to tell Rosso what she saw.

"I'm *certain* that I saw the three of them, as true as you are standing next to me!" she said, making the sign of the cross. "I saw the same men who were following us talking with your friend, Monsieur Villeprieux."

"I just don't understand what it all means," Rosso said as they walked along the crowded lane ways. "How could he know those people? Perhaps it was a coincidence?"

"But then why are those men here, and why was Monsieur talking with them?" she persisted. "He's nice, your friend, but I don't trust him. I don't think he is's what he appears to be. Do be careful Rosso—he's not like you at all."

She stopped in the street.

"Could it be something to do with you coming to Paris, or with your meeting with that Cardinal in Rome?"

"What do you know about that" Rosso asked, surprised, resigning. "That was supposed to be a secret."

She smiled up at him.

"I may not trust Monsieur Villeprieux, but he's right when he says we children see and hear far more than you adults realise."

Laughing, Rosso hurried along the lane, dragging a beaming Clare behind him. He arranged travel by river down the Seine to their final destination, where they would then take a coach to Villeprieux's home. Rosso also found a covered carriage to take them to the wharf.

The driver, a kind man, moved slowly along those pitted streets, knowing that each jolt would disturb the gravely-ill passenger that he carried. They arrived at the wharf, and there he helped install Villeprieux in the most comfortable seat on the barge.

"It was my pleasure to help, Monsieur," he said, refusing Rosso offer of an extra francliver for his kindness.

Villeprieux dozed the way out of Paris and on into the countryside to his home at St Germain en Leys. As the barge drew close to the town, Rosso was unprepared for the sight of the grand Chateau and Church, perched on the high cliffs above the river plain.

"I never knew there were so many palaces and churches in this country of yours" he said out loud.

VIlleprieux stirred from his slumber.

"There is *much* you do not know, my monkish friend. For instance, I omitted to inform you that ma mere is a Countess too. Not that it matters much. My uncle used to say, 'It's not the title that makes the man—it's what's in his heart.' But he was an imbecile and knew nothing of life, really."

He sat up.

"Perhaps I should have been a monk like you, in holy orders, Rosso. Perhaps it would have given me a cause to be less bored by life."

Spent, he slumped back.

"But then, perhaps I'm an imbecile too!" he mused before drifting back to sleep.

When they found a landing, Rosso roused his friend to ask his mother's address. Villeprieux summoned the driver to lean in close, and he whispered the destination to the man, who removed his cap.

"*Oui, Monsieur. Immediatment, Monsieur.*"

Soon, they were on their way from the landing, winding their way up the hillside and out into the country. They had travelled for half an hour when they came to a big wall, which they followed for the next mile. Finally, they came to a gap in the wall, filled with a massive pair of iron gates, held up by two vast limestone pillars, each surmounted with a huge stone eagle. Through the gate, at the end of a seemingly endless driveway, stood a magnificent Chateau, on manicured grounds.

"Tell the porter that the prodigal son has arrived," Villeprieux murmured with a weak wave of his arm from beneath his blankets.

Rosso opened the window and explained who was in the coach and straightway, a messenger was sent ahead to the house. The gates swung open, with a mournful sound coming from the unhappy hinges. The iron shod wheels crunched over the gravel, like an avenging angel grinding its teeth. By the time they reached the main house, a small retinue of servants waited on the steps.

A footman opened the carriage door then another placed a silken footstool by it to ease their descent. When Rosso asked for help with Villeprieux, two more towering gentlemen in resplendent outfits moved as one to help their long absent master up into his old home. Villeprieux glanced up briefly as he mounted the steps and sighed, then he dropped his head, letting his servants lead him to his mother.

The Countess was sitting by the fire, though the weather still retained the warmth of a golden summer's day. She was in the Small Drawing Room, where Rosso thought there was enough room to turn a coach and four and still have room to spare. Flemish tapestries hung on the walls, recounting scenes from the Old Testament. The casement window was closed and heavily draped against the sun outside, in case it should bring a flush to my Lady's chalk-white skin. She sat in regal splendour, whilst the servants made Villeprieux comfortable on the small sofa, now which they drew near to the fire. She showed no emotion, save for a fine tremor of her hands, clasped tightly in her lap. All the while, Rosso and little Clare stood and watched from the safety of the doorway.

After the servants were dismissed, the only sound to be heard in that gloriously padded palace was the crackle from the fire. The Countess turned towards Rosso, seething.

"How *dare* you bring him here in such a condition! What have you *done* to him?"

Villeprieux roused himself.

"Mother dear. Please don't be so boring. That's no way to welcome my guests. What has been going on since I left this mausoleum of a place?"

Pausing, he continued.

"This is my good friend, Brother Rosso. He's a monk, Maman. You see, I have kept good moral company as you so rightly suggested that I should. And the little girl is someone he's trying to help. So do try to be nice to them."

He coughed again, surprised by the foul black fluid that appeared on his kerchief.

"That doesn't look very good," he said with a smile. "Perhaps it'd be better if I retire to my room, Maman. No doubt you will squeeze all the news out of my guests before I reappear."

Maman rang the bell, and the two large retainers carried Villeprieux up to his room. All the while, Rosso and Clare remained where they were. Maman rang the bell once more and summoned a most aloof, yet obviously exulted member of the household.

"You rang, Milady," he said without moving one muscle on his self-controlled face.

"I did, Georges. Please send for the Physician and for the Master's uncle immediately," she said with imperial elegance.

"The matter is already in hand, Milady. Doctor Tremel will be here shortly, but we're led to understand that His Eminence is currently with His royal Highness at the Palace. He may be delayed a little longer."

With the merest hint of a bow, he retreated silently from the drawing room and closed the doors behind him. Still, Rosso and Clare remained quietly by the door.

The Countess seemed to have forgotten them as she sat, staring into the fire, until a log dropped suddenly, shaking her from her reverie.

"Come and sit down here, girl," she said without moving her head.

Clare looked up at Rosso, who nodded his head and the young girl moved up to where the Countess was sitting.

"Sit down," her ladyship said with the mildest tinge of exasperation in her voice. "Why are you here with this monk?"

She looked directly at Clare with a haughty, intimidating stare.

"And don't lie to me girl. I can spot a liar a mile off, and bad things happen to liars!"

Her eyebrows arched, like the black-penciled wings of a hawk, over her flashing green eyes.

A commotion outside the door interrupted her, which was followed by a light tap, a click of the latch, and the appearance of the aloof servant, who seemed mildly discomforted.

"Yes, Georges?" said Milady.

"It's Master Jacques, Milady. He's become a little fractious and is demanding to see a certain Brother Rosso, whom I believe to be *this* gentleman Milady," he said, indicating toward young Rosso.

"Well don't just stand there, monk, you'd better go with him *now!*" the Countess said in a voice that brooked no dissent.

Rosso bowed his head, and glancing at Clare, he was reassured by her quiet confidence. He followed Georges out the room and up a wide sweep of stairs to Villeprieux's room. The floors of the hallway and corridors were flagged, and their walls were draped with tapestries and paintings. A candelabrum hung from the high dome above the stair well, and amongst the jeweled glass were a myriad of candles— such was the size of it.

Rosso was wide-mouthed at the splendor and size of the Countess's Chateau. When he reached the first level, it disappeared in both directions for at least fifty paces.

Loud shouting came from the room at the top of the stairs, and then the sound of smashing glass. When one voice rose above the others, Rosso recognized it, smiling as he entered the room. His smile evaporated when he saw his friend on the bed. Villeprieux as white as the sheets had once been, if it weren't for the black and red vomit that covered them.

At the sight of Rosso, Villeprieux seemed to settle, although rivers of sweat ran down his neck and soaked his nightgown. The servants had tied a white bandage, soaked in ice water, around his head in an effort cool him down. They also cut Villeprieux's hair short, lending the impression that he had been the victim of some terrible assault, or he'd been retrieved from the field of battle.

"Ah, someone whom I can trust at last! Get out, the lot of you! and leave me with my red monk!"

With an energy that came from nowhere her screamed at the servants.

"Get out now! I said: GET OUT!"

The startled staff, so used to the calm clockwork quietness of this stately mansion, scattered in disarray at the sound of his terrible cry.

"Shouting at the staff isn't going to improve your health, Villeprieux," Rosso said, trying to lighten the mood.

"Hopeless! Every last one of them! Hopeless!" Villeprieux gasped, falling back against his pillow.

"What a strange way to die," he said after a few moments, struggling to control his breathing. "No battles! No great fight with a worthy opponent! No maiden's hand to be won! No stranger's life to be saved on a whim!"

In great sadness, he smiled at Rosso.

"Who's talking about anyone dying?" Rosso protested.

Villeprieux glanced at his friend.

"For an honest monk, you're a terrible liar, my friend."

He had barely said the words when he convulsed with another bout of coughing. Rosso went to the bed, holding his friend until the paroxysm had settled. He reached for the jug and poured water on the poultice on Villeprieux's head.

Remarkably, as the water wet the bandage, some coursed down the back of Villeprieux's head, clearing a path through the hair—just as a river in full spate clears all before it. What he saw made Rosso gawk in wonder. On the back of his friend's head, under the matted hair, there was a red, thickened birthmark, in the shape of a butterfly!

Stunned, his mind couldn't cope with all the thoughts that rushed in at the same moment. Another convulsion from Villeprieux shook him out of his confusion, returning him to the present.

Over the next few hours, Villeprieux appeared to settle. Dr Tremel arrived and bled him, which only appeared to make him weaker, though it made the doctor stronger in his conviction.

"It's a humor that young men can catch, but bleeding will help."

The good doctor then retired to the lower drawing room to take some wine with the Countess. When Rosso tried to leave, Villeprieux became more agitated, so Rosso settled and stayed with his friend. He did, though, send a message to see what had become of little Clare.

As the evening sent its silent arms to embrace the day and lead it gently into the peace of night, a calm came over Villeprieux, and the friends began to talk of times gone by.

"Remember the battle?" Villeprieux asked, as if relieved of all his old indolent ways.

"How can anyone forget such carnage as that?" Rosso cringed.

Even as he spoke he could see the gore, smell the blood and hear the screams. In that suspended moment, it seemed to them that dead men came back to life and all the pain that they'd ever experienced was immediate.

"I came back to look for you," said Villeprieux.

After a pause to mop his friend's brow, Rosso nodded.

"I know. Agnes told me someone was with me, but they left. But in my heart, I always knew it was you."

"It was probably the only noble thing I ever did in my life," Villeprieux said, his closed eyes presently tinged with blue.

In the silence that followed, Rosso was loath to speak. He listened to his friend's calm breathing, thinking that perhaps the dreadful fever would pass, just as the good physician had predicted.

"Did you ever father any children?" Rosso asked.

"Yes," Villeprieux replied. "There *was* a child—such a long time ago now, though. Sometimes, I've thought that I should have kept her," he said in his old distracted manner.

"But uncle took care of all that. You see, uncle is very good at taking care of those sorts of things. It's his job, burying all those bodies the rest of us don't want anything to do with."

He lapsed again into silence.

✠ ✠ ✠

In the early hours of the morning, Rosso, slumbering in the chair that he placed next to the bed, awakened from his dreams. His friend was coughing violently, and with each cough, the black fluid became redder. Rosso called for help, and Dr Tremel appeared. With the arrogance of an implied knowledge, the doctor summed up the situation in an instant and began to let more blood from the dying man's arm.

Villeprieux became whiter, while a fine sweat covered his face. His strength, quickly ebbing, he turned toward Rosso.

"I'm not the true friend you think me to be, dear Rosso."

Rosso vehemently deflected such a "foolish thought."

"You see, dear Rosso, in this life of ours—all I saw was a wonderful game to play, and I played them all. These games I played—they had no flavour no lasting taste, and in the end, they bored me."

There was such sadness, such exhaustion in his voice as he spoke.

"But then along comes a Rosso, or a Gino, or even the poor Dom, and the game makes no sense anymore."

He paused to catch his breath.

"You know what, Rosso? You opened a door and let a chink of light into my dark places."

He closed his eyes again as his pulse, which was once robust and full of life, raced like a fragile thread through his body.

"Villeprieux," Rosso whispered into the dying man's ear. "Can you still hear me?"

The Frenchman squeezed his friend's hand, but his eyes never moved.

"Villeprieux—remember that child you once *had*? I *know* who she is."

He opened his eyes, smiling gently.

"*You* know her too," Rosso pressed. "Her name is Clare…"

A soft, healing tear ran from the corner of Jacques Villeprieux's eye, blessing his pale face. Then he closed his eyes for the very last time.

His mother had never once visited him whilst he was ill, but she arrived in the doorway after news of his death.

"Leave me alone with my son," she told the servants. They hurried out, and then Rosso, last of all, left her to mourn her son.

When she descended the stairway some time later, there was no trace of grief or mourning in her face, her voice or her demeanor.

"Is there any news of his uncle?" she asked Georges, before returning to her place by the fire in the drawing room.

Clare found Rosso sitting on the steps outside, watching the light of dawn march with gathering confidence, the coloring the countryside. Life stirred everywhere. Swallows flew out from their nooks beneath the eaves and busy bees sought the pollen in the dew-laden flowers.

As she sat next to him, he put his arm around her little shoulders to guard her from the damp of the morning.

"It's funny out here," she said without looking up. "It all *looks* so beautiful, and yet your friend lies dead in the bed upstairs."

Rosso patted her shoulder as he felt his tired gritty eyes grow blurry in the newly-born sunshine.

"Did you know the Countess was his Maman?" she asked in innocence.

"Yes, and no" he said. "Yes, Villeprieux had told me something about her, but no, I never knew she was a Countess, and I'd never met her before."

"I think she's very sad, really," Clare said.

Rosso looked down with an inquiring look.

"Mmm. She didn't talk much about him, she just asked me lots of questions about who I was and who you were, but when I talked about your friend, she never took her eyes off me. It was if she was trying to see something that she'd missed."

She looked up at Rosso.

"She pretends to be a very scary lady, but underneath all that iciness, she has a kind heart."

Clare spoke her final words with the supreme confidence that only a young girl could.

Rosso squeezed her shoulders.

"You're one very wise young lady, Mademoiselle Clare. You scare me!"

The appearance of a coach on the gravel drive as it raced toward the house interrupted their moment of quiet intimacy. His Eminence, Cardinal Villeprieux, descended before anyone could aid him, and he moved swiftly toward the Chateau.

"I *pray* that I'm not too late!" he said with the consternation showing in his voice.

It took only Rosso's avoiding his gaze for him to understand that he was. He stopped where he was, grasping the Crucifix hanging on a silvered chain around his neck, and he covered his eyes with his other hand.

After composing himself, he ascended the final steps, walked straight past the travelers and in through the open door, his crimson cape creating coruscations amongst the unswept leaves.

"I think we'd better stay here," Rosso said. "No doubt they'll call us when they want us."

They had only made one round of the grand fountain at the entrance of the Chateau before Georges appeared to announce, without any emotion, that Brother Rosso was expected by his Eminence in the library, and would Mademoiselle Clare care to join the staff below stairs to break her fast.

It was more an order than a request, and both returned to the house, headed separate ways under his imperious gaze.

✛ ✛ ✛

The library was dark and poorly-lit, with just a few guttering candles. The room had gained its reputation from the vellum manuscripts it contained. The magnificently illustrated books, purchased or stolen from some distant potentate, were on display on gloriously carved lecterns, each one of which was a work of art.

The Cardinal was leafing his way through one of these books.

"This is from the Old Testament," he said, pausing to read a few verses.

"What apocalyptic stuff that was," he muttered to himself. "Not many signs of God's loving redemption there—war, revenge, an eye for an eye…"

He trailed off into silence. Then looking up, he spoke gently to Rosso.

"Do you think we've *learned* anything since Abraham walked the earth? Was this all in vain?"

He grasped his crucifix and thrust it in Rosso's direction.

"Little matter," he continued. "Tell me all you can about my nephew's illness?"

"Your nephew?" cried Rosso. "But you told me you didn't know him! You *lied* to me!"

The Cardinal's tired eyes gazed at the young monk, and the falling sound of a sheaf of vellum pages was the only sound that disturbed the silence.

"Truth? What is truth? Do you remember who said that, Brother Rosso? Pontius Pilate! I'm in the unfortunate position of having to judge people, just as he did. And just like that poor frightened potentate in that remote, fly-blown part of the Roman Empire, even an eminent Cardinal can make mistakes."

He reached out both of his hands spoke simply.

"Forgive me."

Rosso felt embarrassed and angry, but above all, he recognized a fellow human who was suffering.

"I forgive you, your Eminence," he said softly, and they both embraced. "But there's much I don't know about your nephew. Was it really an accident that we met on our journey here, or had he planned it? Clare told me she saw him with two men who had chased us earlier, and whom we believed to have been Spanish spies."

"Ahh," said the older man. "You loved my nephew, and yet you doubted him too. Your loyally overcame your fears, and that's both a strength and a weakness in a man. No doubt, you'll have learned from that, and in the future, you'll be a wiser and more cautious man. But Jacques was a feckless creature in many respects. Some said he took after his father— my elder brother before him."

"I'd known of Jacques presence ever since he arrived in Italy. You see, even I have friends who are loyal to me, and who help me by gathering useful information."

"*Spies*, you mean, Eminence?" Rosso interjected.

"Call them what you will," his Eminence replied. "But do allow me to continue. You remember that battle you told me about? Well Jacques did escape, but that was only with the connivance of the Spanish. As you'll recall, he had been parlaying with them—even though he was in the pay of the Florentines.

"He frequently sold his talents—and what prodigious talents they were—to the highest bidder. In this case, the highest bidder happened to be Spanish. Perhaps those talents might have been put to better use if only he'd been better guided as a child."

The Cardinal paused to snuffed out a struggling candle, replacing it with another, unconsciously making a sign of the cross as he lit it.

"So, when Jacques got wind of a secret deal between the Pope and the French King, he smelt money and sold himself to the Spanish again. Somewhere along the line, he changed his mind and he left them at Lyon. Perhaps he'd finally discovered that loyalty was real, after all. I hope he did. The rest of the story, well—you know better than I."

"So why was I sent from Rome to meet you here in France? No one gave me any message to bring. All I was told was to find you and make contact with you," Rosso asked, still puzzled.

"There was no *written* message," the Cardinal said, smiling for the first time. "That was the beauty and the simplicity of it all. You were the message! His Holiness was either going to say yes or no to the French proposal, and you were one of those answers. We had arranged for one of two monks to come to Paris— one with *black* hair and the other with…"

His voice trailed off.

"Well that's pretty obvious to you now, isn't it? Black monk and Red monk—each one signifing either *yes* or *no*. It was as simple as that."

"Well which one was I?" Rosso begged.

The Cardinal smiled once more.

"Ah, now that would be giving state secrets away, and I couldn't do that, could I? Now, tell me a little more of the child you brought with you. I'm intrigued. It seems to me to be a very strange thing to drag a poor child halfway across the continent—especially as the companion of an Augustinian monk. So there must be something more to that story than meets my humble eye."

Rosso hesitated for a moment. There stood a man of great power, and one whose presence would make most tremble—but he'd just asked a humble monk to forgive him, so Rosso decided to step out in faith and hope to the highest heavens that he hadn't made a huge mistake.

Taking a deep breath, he told the story of young Clare, and how he believed that she was in fact Villeprieux's lost daughter. The only reaction that he got from his Eminence was a whitening of his knuckles as he gripped the edge of the lectern in front of him. Then relaxing, a little he invited Rosso to take a chair.

"Because I want to tell you a fairytale…"

Rosso sat, watching the Cardinal closely while listening to the story he told.

"Imagine a young man, full of vigor and heir to a great fortune. Imagine that his father was too proud of his son, and he spoiled him with gifts and treasures. Imagine that the son was a leader of men, and the men loved him in return. Then consider that the son had many weaknesses of character too. He gambled and wenched, and his word was of no more worth than the empty wine skins he left behind in the taverns and brothels.

"He had a younger brother, a more timid yet serious youth who was frightened by the sound of metal on metal, who blanched at the sight of his own blood. Yet he loved and worshiped his elder brother.

"A marriage of great convenience was arranged for the elder boy, which increased the wealth and power of the family. But war came and the young man, ignoring his father's wishes, joined the King to fight for the Holy Roman Emperor at the borders of the realm.

"Back at home, the younger brother was left with the young, isolated bride. They liked each other and were often in each other's company. Time and loneliness drove them into each other's arms, and they became lovers. The elder brother returned briefly and sensed the change in them both. Laughing in their faces he shouted, 'You scum! I can pick up a hundred like you any time I want,' and in the next day he left. Not long after, the report came that he was killed in battle, but as time went on, stories circulated that he'd died over a gambling debt in some sordid tavern in Paris. It matters not—remember this is but a fairytale!

"Soon, a child was born, and he was named Jacques, after his father, and everyone grieved for the widowed bride and her newborn son. The dead man's younger brother, filled with remorse, entered holy orders and advanced rapidly to high office within the Curia of the Church. What more can that man of Holy orders do, but the little good that he can for his son, and perhaps his granddaughter too?"

There Cardinal Villeprieux, father to Jacques Villeprieux fell silent. Rosso, who had not uttered a sound throughout this whole dialogue, nervously broke the silence.

"So who is Clare's mother, then?"

As the Cardinal turned, his face was as expressionless as a marbled statue.

"You must never ask that question, Brother Rosso. To do so would put all our lives at risk. You must never ask me again."

He relaxed his tone.

"Take the little girl back to where she really belongs—to Rome. She will be loved there. I have people who will contact you from time to time, and should things change, then I'll get a message to you. I trust you to take good care of my grandchild."

"But the Countess?" Rosso pleaded.

"Ah yes," the Cardinal said, taping the front of his chest.

"In my heart, I never stopped loving her. But something froze in her when my brother died, and things were never quite the same. If you know Jacques, then you know his mother. She can be charming and generous, but…"

He paused, searching for the right words

"She's not always consistent in her manner or her actions. Yes, she'd love the child for a time, and then she'd tire of her and replace that love with gifts. Her inconsistencies would lead the poor child into a nightmare of absences and indulgences, and that, Brother Rosso, I will not permit."

Carefully closing the book in front of him, he invited Rosso to leave the room with him.

✣ ✣ ✣

Riding away from the chateau in a carriage provided for them by His Eminence, Rosso and Clare sat in silence, surrounded by the memories of all that had happened in such a short time.

"What happened back there?" Clare asked in her wise little voice. "Did you deliver you message?"

"Sort of," Rosso mused. "Let me just say that it was one of the funniest messages I've ever delivered."

He smiled at his own secret joke.

"You look funny when you smile like that," Clare said. "The Cardinal has a funny smile like that, too. It's when you think I don't understand, but I do. You had to do something very secret and very important, and he's such a very important person, and he's got to keep lots of secrets too. And somehow, Jacques Villeprieux was very important and a very special secret between both of you."

Rosso continued to look out of the window, afraid that if he looked at her, she would see all the answers written on his face.

"But one secret we didn't solve," he said while still looking out at the receding chateau, "is who your parents were."

"Hmm," said Clare, "I think I *know*."

Startled, Rosso turned, staring into her eyes.

"Tell me little sister. Who do you think they were?"

"Well, it's not so much of who they were, but who they are," she said softly.

Taking Rosso's hand, she continued.

"You remember when you first found me and took me to Marco and Laura's home—and Sara and her brothers played with me so normally in the garden—and me, a total stranger, and not a very nice one at that? And do you remember how I was so rude to Marco when he just tried to be nice to me? Well…"

She broke off for a moment, remembering the distant past.

"I think you know what I mean about men who call themselves your father, but are no more than horrible beasts to you. But then *you* came along, and then Marco—who was so patient with me, and so loving and so, so very gentle. *That's* why when I talk about who my parents are, I always think of them because they are the only parents I've ever really known. Do you think they would ever take me back?" she asked.

Rosso smiled in that sacred moment, putting his arms around her.

"Why don't we go and *ask* them?"

About the Author

*"I spent all my life learning the rules. Now that I know
which ones are irrelevant, life is simpler!"*

AFTER MORE THAN thirty years as a busy family
practice physician in Perth, Duncan Jefferson retired from
his practice and started traveling. He still practices medicine
part time, as a relief doctor traveling to the most remote
corners of Australia, and in between assignments he and
his wife travel the world.

DUNCAN HAS WALKED THE FAMOUS CAMINO DE SANTIAGO, AND
NOW VOLUNTEERS HIS TIME AS THE CHAIRMAN OF THE PILGRIM

TrailFoundation,whichisorganizingasimilar,contem-plative-stylewalkinAustraliacalledtheCaminoSalvado.

Visit him online at

WWW.DUNCANJEFFERSON.COM